If You'd Like to Make a Call, Please Hang Up

- Stories -

Bob Thurber

D1468751

ISBN: 9781679392528

Cover design by Sam Thurber, SMT Design.

Other books by Bob Thurber:

Cinderella She Was Not: A Novelette
Nickel Fictions: 50 Exceedingly Brief Stories
Nothing by Trouble: Stories and Images (with Vincent Louis Carrella)
Paperboy: A Dysfunctional Novel
In Fifty Words! Microfictions

https://scanticbooks.blogspot.com
Facebook: Scantic Books

Table of Contents

Foreword

I've known Bob Thurber since I met him online in 1999, in the Zoetrope Writer's Workshop. I read a story of his, "All Set for Ardor?" and I gave it an ecstatic review. I said that parts reminded me of Hemingway. Not the faux-Hemingway style—the real Hemingway.

Bob replied to my review. We began to talk. We became friends.

I never wavered in my regard for Bob's work. I was not surprised to find that he writes constantly on scraps of paper. That he has a trunk full of unpublished work. That he spends many hours on a single sentence.

To me, Bob Thurber is Hemingway. Maybe he is even more than Hemingway. There is truth in his work—more truth than it seems anybody should be able to handle (least of all, Bob himself; yet, miraculously, with the attentive hand and keen though dimming eye of an Old Master, he does handle it).

If you are holding this book, prepare to be ravished and shattered by the brushwork of this man I personally regard as the Rembrandt of short fiction in our all too slick and cynical time.

- Andrew L. Wilson, Author and Editor-at Large

The Next Stop

"And the end of all our exploring will be to arrive where we started and know the place for the first time." – T.S. Eliot

The place looked neither deserted nor open. It was a cable-car-style restaurant with a long row of windows, and a small boxy addition attached. No cars, no movement, no hint of life, no reason to stop. The sun was glaring off the glass; the vents on the roof sparkled like silver.

I can't speak for my companions but I wasn't hungry, though none of us had eaten for days. I forget who was driving, whose turn it was. It might have been me. We had worked out a system, a timed rotation that was far more complex than it needed to be for five people. Whomever was behind the wheel, he slowed us down and we idled at the lot's edge, the car parallel with the highway. We studied the building, looking for rain barrels or anything that might hold water.

"The sign just flickered," one of us said.

"It's just the sun," someone answered.

"No. I saw it, too," said another.

"Maybe someone saw us pull in," said the first man.

"There. See? It flickered again."

"I bet it's a signal."

"A signal for what," I said.

"Or a warning," somebody answered.

"We should go in," said the first man.

There was no talking to any of them. Hope does terrible things to people. Apparently they had forgotten that the sun had been playing tricks on us for a thousand miles.

Then someone read the name of the place out loud, stressing the consonants, stretching the syllables, saying it over and over, making what was printed on that sign sound like the lyrics to a song or a mantra that would eventually bring transcendence to us all.

Then we were all saying it the same way, and that was enough to get us squirming in our seats, each taking a turn looking at another while we mouthed the name over and over. No one wanted to be the first out of the car, the first shadow to stretch across that crushed stone lot, pointing toward more disappointment.

From the beginning a big part of our problem was that we lacked a true leader.

"Let's all go in together," I said quietly.

I wasn't a take charge guy but I'm ninety-percent sure it was me who said it, though it's possible we all vocalized the same thought at the same time. Our throats were dry and our lungs were so full of dust that our collective voices would have barely exceeded a whisper. And what's funny about that, pretty near ironic, is we had all at one time made a decent living with our voices, either in front of a class room, or at a podium, or on a theatrical stage, or, in my case, from inside a glass enclosed office perched high above an assembly line.

I blame the heat. I'm still fuzzy about what was said, what was implied, how long we sat there staring at what might have been salvation, immediate destruction, or both. I'm probably not the best person to tell this story. Though, I can say with absolute certainty that none of us got out.

I think part of what held our attention so long was that the sun had turned the windows into a row of mirrors, and in some of those mirrors our reflections were looking at us like people inside looking out. And those were the people we wanted to be, and would have become if we weren't such miserable cowards.

Before we drove off I took a mental snapshot to hang on the wall surrounding my heart. Soon the sun would be gone and the road would no longer waver like the surface of an endless black river. Soon only our headlights would guide us, and the moon's glow, if there was a moon, would try to help. I wasn't worried. I had an innate sense of optimism that I couldn't shake, and I knew that together, sooner or later, we would get somewhere, and we'd know it the moment we arrived.

Beauty Takes Care of Itself

Six weeks out of rehab, just when things were beginning to turn around for me, I woke up stiff and sore on a park bench with the sun glaring from the worst possible angle. Curled tight on my side, with no notion how I'd gotten there, all I could hear were the squeaks and squawks of early morning birds. That shrill noise, combined with the blinding light, knotted such pressure behind my eyes that it took me a full minute to fully focus and realize the racket wasn't birds but children.

Crowded around me, twitching and chattering, were a dozen girls in sparkly, colorful dresses, all with garish makeup and complicated hairdos. They looked like Munchkins dressed for the prom.

Someone said, "Ladies, please!"

It was a man's voice, thick and deep. Fearing it was a cop, I sat up. The girls shrieked and scattered.

"Whoa, ladies!" the man said.

He was crouched behind a camera mounted on a tripod. "Great. You woke him. Nice job." He removed his hand from the lens and stepped forward. He had long hair and a short beard. His arms were bare beneath a puffy vest with a dozen pockets. "Take five, ladies. Nobody go anywhere."

"Where's the bathroom?" said one of the girls.

They had gathered into groups like teams huddling before a play. I felt sorry for them. Their pale necks appeared too delicate to support their embellished heads.

"Hold your water until we're back at the bus," the man said, coming straight at me. His slanted expression distorted the shape of his beard; his baggy camouflage pants and rope sandals made him look like a commando Jesus. I avoided eye contact by staring at the girls. Faces peeked; whispers and giggles erupted in waves.

"They're something, aren't they?" the man said, leaning uncomfortably close. "They're the finalists. We're supposed to be shooting over at the zoo but they're experiencing some kind of monkey problem. Dead baby chimp, I suspect." His shadow provided a softer view of the girls. "I'm breaking the rules shooting here. Meanwhile, I've got two worthless chaperones back on the bus, rubbing coconut oil on their feet."

A big-eyed blonde, inches taller than the rest, timidly twirled her index fingers into the hollows of her cheeks. Without raising my arm I wiggled my fingers in reply. "What's your name, sweetheart?" I said loudly.

"Bernard," the man said. "People call me Bernie."

"I wasn't talking to you," I said.

"I'm sure you weren't, but I'd still like to shake your hand."

He extended his arm. An oversized, complex-looking watch crowded his wrist.

"Introduce me to that really pretty one," I said. "Then I'll shake your hand."

"No can do, I'm afraid." He sat down beside me. It was a long bench, big enough for four people unless any of them were fat.

"How old?" I said.

He hesitated. "Most are nine, some are eight."

"They look older. Especially her." I pointed at the one I wanted to take home. She was staring intently, like we were in some kind of contest. I strained not to blink. She seemed to be wearing less makeup than the rest. Finally, she blinked, or rather her eyelids fluttered, and her mouth broke into a shy, radiant smile.

"What are you thinking?" Bernie or Bernard said.

Believing my immediate thoughts none of his business, I said, "They remind me of those fancy French pastries, all fluffy inside, but ruined by too much frosting."

"Oh, they're a sugary bunch, alright." He shifted his feet. "Unfortunately half these darlings will outgrow their cuteness, turn out mildly attractive at best. The true beauties will do okay, finish college, marry into money, live comfortably ever after. Because beauty takes care of itself. But most are headed for a lifetime of self-image problems, self-esteem issues, depression, eating disorders." He shook his head in a self-congratulatory sort of way. "Statistically speaking, at least three will end up shallow, vain, heartless bitches."

"Yummy," I said viciously.

"Megan has an underdeveloped bladder," shouted one of the girls.

"No. No. That's not what I said!"

"I'm bored," said another girl.

"Two seconds," Bernie said. "Stop bickering." He stood. "You homeless?"

I turned my face. "Do I look homeless?"

"Honestly," he said, "It's hard to tell."

The sun was giving his head a fierce, dazzling glow.

"No, I'm not homeless."

"I would have guessed the opposite."

The pretty blonde touched three fingers to her mouth, puffed her cheeks and blew a kiss.

"Listen," Bernie said, leaning closer. "Before they woke you I shot maybe a dozen frames. I don't know what I've got, if there's anything I can use, but do you want to sign a release?"

"No."

"Good. I don't have the forms with me. Can I offer you some cash?"

"How much?"

"Twenty bucks?"

I nodded.

"Super!" He unzipped a vest pocket and reached in. He pressed a folded bill into my hand and said, "Nice doing business with you."

I watched him jog to his camera, collapse the tripod's legs and hoist the thing onto his shoulder. I fought the urge to call him back. My jaw was clenched so tight it hurt my ears. He quickly caught up to the group, then hurried past them, signaling like a cavalry leader charging into battle.

I swung my feet up and stretched out, proud of myself for not pulling my daughter's picture from my wallet, for not blurting out how I'd lost the precious darling to a vindictive ex-wife in a drawn-out custody battle, all because some dumb judge believed her ugly lies.

At the rehab center they have a courtyard with a stone chapel—a small, friendly space with two stained-glass windows and a few pine benches, where, on rainy days, patients were allowed to smoke. I'd sometimes sit and contemplate God's misjudgment of the world, all his miscalculations and bumbling oversights, convinced that any Divine Plan in no way included deadbeat dads or the devils who made them.

If You'd Like to Make a Call, Please Hang Up

At ten minutes to midnight Dean stepped out of an airport taxi with a stuffed panda the size of an easy chair. He set the bear on the roof of the cab and looked beyond the ragged and overgrown hedges fronting his one-story house. He scanned the windows, checking for movement and light, then he turned his attention to the windows of the neighboring houses. He steadied the Panda with one hand and scratched at four day's worth of beard. While the cabdriver jotted something on a clipboard, Dean leaned on the taxi's open door; he worked his fingernails into the flesh beneath his beard as he studied the cars parked along the street. The driver said something. Dean startled, but made no reply as he reconsidered the front of his house. After a long moment he leaned into the cab and reached across the back seat for an aluminum baseball bat. The bat was wrapped in a cellophane skin. The woman at the gift shop had stuck a flattened blue bow over the price tag. Dean pulled his head out of the taxi and breathed in a mouthful of air. He set the bat across the bear's legs.

The driver said, "We all set here, sir?"

Dean picked at a loop of ribbon, stretching the bow back to its original shape. Then he closed the rear door of the cab and stepped up to the driver's window. He smiled cockeyed and showed the man five fingers. "You wait. Okay? Ten, at most," Dean said. Then he took out his wallet and paid twice the fare. "Don't go anywhere, I mean it," he told the driver.

While the driver counted his money, Dean secured the bear in a headlock. He walked around the rear of the taxi, then up the driveway to the garage. He pressed his face against a window square, caught a glimpse of bare cement floor. Wielding the bat like a machete, he pushed through the high hedges bordering the driveway.

The sky was clear and the moon was full. Dean watched the windows as he circled the house. He listened to the crickets and to the swishing sound his trousers made in the tall grass. The rear porch light was on and the new key was in the window box. It was hard fitting the key in the lock until he put the bear down.

He used the bat to bump the door open. The moon forced his shadow across the floor, but he waited a ten count, listening, before he stepped into the kitchen, bear first. Seconds later the babysitter snapped on the overhead light. She put a hand to her mouth. Dean raised the bat and stepped forward. But then he recognized her, and she must have recognized him, even with the beard, because she didn't scream.

She was a skinny girl with long flat hair and a pimply chin. She apologized for being half-asleep. Her braces glittered as she smiled at the huge bear. She puffed out her chest, then smiled at Dean. Twirling the ends of her hair, she told him she knew everything, the whole story, but that it didn't matter. Not to her, anyway. She said as far as she was concerned Dean was still Billy's father. She said she respected that.

She went on to tell Dean a short tale about her own father, a man she'd never met. Dean stroked the point of his beard and listened to every word.

When she was through talking, Dean handed her twenty dollars and told her to gather her things. He said the ride home was on him, a bonus for doing such an outstanding job. At the front door he concentrated on her hips as she angled across the lawn. From the cab's window she called, "Welcome back, Mr. Forester," and she waved the twenty like a tiny flag.

After the taxi pulled away Dean looked in on Billy. The hall light sliced across the wallpaper, a baseball pattern set against a sea of green. Above the bed a book shelf crowded with small trophies cast slanted shadows.

Dean leaned the bat against a desk near the door. He put the bear on the bed, between the boy and the wall. He lifted a Red Sox cap off the bedpost and set it on the bear's huge head. He made some adjustments—to the bear, to the hat, to the collar of Billy's pajamas. Then he sat on the bed, on the very edge, knees together, and stroked the boy's hair.

After a minute of this, he stood up and tapped out a cigarette from the pack he'd bought at the airport. He clenched the cigarette between his teeth but didn't light it. He watched the boy sleep. He watched the sheet move up and down with the boy's breathing.

Dean paced for a while, staying within the border of an oval rug. He paced and he pretended to smoke the unlit cigarette.

Finally, from the inside pocket of his blazer, Dean brought out his copy of the restraining order. He angled the paper to catch the light, then moved it high and away to avoid his own shadow. As he read, he hummed part of a tune the taxi driver had played over and over on a trunk-sized cassette player. Dean hummed very softly. The cigarette wagged in his mouth. Then he put the paper away and reached down to smooth the boy's hair again.

He made a slight adjustment to the cap on the bear's head, then he lit the cigarette and smoked, watching the boy, pulling long slow puffs, turning away only to exhale.

Dean flicked ashes into his palm. When the cigarette had burned down he crossed the hall and emptied his hand over the toilet bowl. Bent low beneath the mirror he washed in the sink, squeezing the flower-shaped soap into a featureless ball. He used the towel monogrammed HIS, then carried it into the hallway. He closed Billy's door, rolled the towel hand over fist, turned, pump faked once, and shot the towel into the sink.

In the kitchen, he shut off the overhead light. Then he shut off the porch floodlights. The second he did, moonlight streamed onto the glossy cabinets and powdery walls. He admired the fall of shadows in the quiet kitchen for a moment then opened the porch door and put the key back in the window box. He heard a car on the street beyond the redwood fence. Dean squinted at the spaces between the houses in that direction, then he closed the door and hurried into the dining room. He stood away from the curtains and looked out. There were street lights and an occasional window light that gave the neighboring houses a soft glow. He watched the headlights approach, counted four heads as the car slowly passed. Then he stepped closer to the window and followed the taillights until the car turned off. He went back to the kitchen and opened the fridge. He moved some things around—a jug of milk, a carton of eggs, a sticky jar of strawberry jam. He pushed aside a sealed Tupperware bowl and read the label on a long thin-necked bottle of vinaigrette. From the bottom shelf he took out an L-shaped slab of sheet-cake with green frosting and a half-dozen small figures in various baseball poses. He pulled out one of the figures, licked the frosting from its spike, then stabbed the figure back in. He slid the cake into the fridge and closed the door.

In the den the TV flickered quietly in a corner. He sat on the sofa and fingered his beard. There were pretzels in a bowl beside the phone and he took one. It was fat as a cigar. He crunched it between his back teeth, found the remote and shut off the TV. When his shoulders started to tremble, he put his chin down. He stroked his beard and picked lint from his trousers while he waited to cry. He could feel himself filling up.

The phone rang and he jolted upright. He lifted the receiver to his ear but didn't say anything. There was music, muddled voices, part of a drum roll. He heard a woman shriek, then a sharp click and the music stopped.

Dean hung up the phone but kept his hand on the receiver. While he waited, he moved a magazine with a yellow-haired guitar player on the slick cover. Someone had used a sharp pen to carve a heart shape around the guitar player's head. Dean traced the image with his thumbnail until the phone rang again.

This time, above the thumping music, came his wife's voice.

"Edna? Hello? Edna, it's Vivian."

Dean held his breath.

"Edna?" the caller said.

Over the music a man's voice broke in, "Earth to Edna, come in Edna!"

"Stop it," Vivian said. "Let go. Will you let go?"

When the music stopped Dean listened to the silence for a while then he rested the receiver on the pretzel bowl. He lit a cigarette and blew smoke at the phone. Somewhere outside, a dog barked.

Dean flicked ashes into the bowl. He stroked his beard and looked at the window. When a faint voice said, "If you'd like to make a call, please hang up ..." Dean stuffed the receiver deep between the sofa cushions.

He stayed on the couch, chain smoking, and using the bowl as an ashtray. At one point, he pushed the heart-shape through the magazine's cover. Then he held the open magazine to his face, blew smoke rings through the hole. When he heard a car's motor, he pulled one last hit into his lungs, then crushed the cigarette onto a pretzel.

He hurried down the hall to Billy's room. He stepped inside and closed the door. The boy was using one leg of the stuffed bear as a pillow. From the other room he heard voices. Then he heard his wife: "We're back. Edna! Edna, we're home!"

A man's voice echoed, "Edna!"

Dean removed his blazer and hung it on a bed post.

"If she went home and left him ... I swear ... So help me God."

"Chill out," the man said.

"Edna!"

Dean stood with his ear to the door and his eyes on the boy. He rolled his shirt sleeves and listened to the two of them call out together.

"Probably making out with the pizza boy," said the man. "Check our room."

Dean fingered his beard. He watched the light beneath the door.

"I smell smoke," his wife said.

Dean heard the clack of heels on hardwood.

"Russ. Russ, I smell smoke."

"Easy, Viv! Don't pull on me. You'll tear open my stitches."

Then he said, "What do you make of this."

There was a short silence, then Vivian said, "Edna doesn't smoke."

"Then who," the man said.

Dean picked up the bat. "I don't know who. But those are not Edna's."

"Let's find out.," the man said. "Hey Edna! Come out, come out, wherever you are."

Dean heard his wife say, "Russ wait. Let's call the police."

"For what? We don't know anything. You hunt for sleeping beauty. I'll check on DiMaggio Junior."

"Russ, wait," the woman said.

Dean slapped the bow off the handle. He adjusted his grip then rested the barrel against his shoulder.

"Daddy?"

Dean didn't turn, didn't look at the boy. He strained to hear the voices in the hall.

"Is it still my birthday, Daddy?"

"Hey Billy," Dean whispered. "Hey sport." He cocked his elbow, set his stance. "Close your eyes a minute, son."

Blue Light

My father was up, pacing in the shadows. The whole house was dark except for a hall lamp. Through the archway I saw the red dot of his cigarette floating above the piano. I hooked my shoes on the strap of my bag, shut the door soft, then headed for the stairs. I was wearing one of mom's summer dresses and I had dribbled tequila on the front; I didn't want to get into anything over ruining old clothes.

"Not so fast, Missy."

I wasn't moving very fast or very well. With my hair pinned up off my neck I suddenly felt chilled to the bone, and a lot less steady than I'd felt getting out of Robert's family mini-van. Robert was a child. I was a two time college dropout dating a high school junior on the basketball team and the whole town knew.

Dad moved into the light but I kept going.

"Hey. Whoa. Hold on a minute."

I slid forward on the tiles. I dropped my bag, a shoe went flying. He got to the stairs before I did, stopped me from tumbling head-first into the rail. He straightened me up, held me awkwardly beneath my breasts a moment, then made himself big and blew smoke at my head.

"Inside," he said.

He guided me two robot steps in the right direction, but when he took his hands away I turned back. I frowned at his feet. He was barefoot like me.

"What is it," he said.

"I'm going to be sick," I said.

"You're not going to be sick. Go in and sit down. Quick pow wow."

I swayed a little and tried to stay focused on his feet. They had the same shape as mine, the same toes, except my nails were painted cherry-red. He raised my chin with one finger. He had the cigarette dangling from the side of his mouth like a TV detective.

He squinted. "Did you have sex with a minor tonight, Miss?"

I snarled a blubbery noise. "You're not funny."

He said, "Yes, I am. Your boyfriend's mother called. I made her laugh so hard she agreed to drop all charges."

"I'm tired, Daddy. And a tiny wee bit drunk."

"Sleep is for sissies," he said. "And if you're more drunk than me you're grounded."

He grasped my shoulders and turned me slow. He said, "I need your help with the TV again."

I faked a foot stomping fit. "I need sleep, daddy. Sleep sleep sleep."

"No one needs sleep. That's a lazy man's myth."

He was behind me, sniffing. Pulling deep breaths from the air around me. I imagined he could smell the scents of my evening, where I'd been, the food I'd touched, what I'd smoked, and the thick smell of Robert, the handsome child with the body of a man, the boy who only said he loved me when I had his dick in my hand.

"Step inside my parlor," my father said. "I won't keep you very long from dreaming your precious dreams about your beautiful Robert."

"Dad. Please. Work. Remember. Early."

"Move it," he said.

"I can't. I'm up and out of here in less than four hours."

He puffed up a little. "Whose fault is that? That's not my fault."

He motioned me toward the big chair.

"Have a seat, Missy."

"Promise me this has nothing to do with mom. Promise me and I'll help. Because it's three a.m. and I love you Daddy, but I don't have the strength."

He patted my bum. "Be my guest," he said.

I dragged my feet across the carpet; the new TV snapped on. The giant screen was blue, soundless. Ghostly shapes took form in the haze. I watched the picture roll, then drop back into the frame. I fell into his big chair and sat straight back to hide my face between the wings. The cushions felt warm against my thighs and back.

"Tell me why's it doing that," my father said.

He stepped across my view, waving the remote as though directing an orchestra. The sleek new TV was a used model, an eBay auction bargain that had cost twice the bidding price to ship from Canada. It had more features than a Sears microwave oven. On screen a highlighted bar flickered through a list of menu options.

My father cursed.

In the background the picture rolled and snapped, rolled and snapped.

"What did you do?" I said. "Tell me everything you did after I went out."

"Nothing. Not a thing," he said. "Not at first. Then I started getting green fuzzy edges so I hit the auto program and this is what I got."

"What else?"

"Then I pushed other things. I couldn't get a menu."

"What did you push? Tell me everything."

"Hell knows what I didn't push. This keypad is like a science calculator," he said. "So far I missed two heavyweight fights. Right now I'm missing bikini babes running a carwash business. Do you think it's the way we've got it wired?"

I had settled deep into the corner of his chair. I was sunk in, hugging myself.

I said, "Another tiny reason why a users manual is nice to have."

He said, "I unplugged it twice but it won't reset. There must be a battery."

I closed my eyes, then quickly opened them. "Is it true I used to sleep here?" I said snuggling up like I was going to snooze.

My father crawled past me on his hands and knees. He stopped two feet in front of the TV screen. "Long time since you slept there. A different life then. Your mother lived on that couch, because of her back. All she did was watch TV. First years of your life that was mostly your bed."

I could feel myself going, starting to drift.

"I think I remember some of that. I don't remember sleeping straight through the night in this chair. I should remember. I dream a lot about sleep."

"Not your mother, though. Never your mother. And not that chair. One just like it though," my father said.

I sat up, leaned towards the light. The brightness cast a blue glare on my father's face. He had his hands apart, measuring.

"God, you were such a tiny thing, you'd fit lying down, straight out. Every last inch of you."

"I was a good baby, wasn't I, Daddy?"

He thumped the TV with his fist. "You were an angel." He banged the set again; the picture popped and rattled. "You just outgrew it, like everything else."

Belly Breathing

August and hot. Miserable heat. The air's too thick to breathe, never mind prance around in a ratty wig and face paint. I'm pacing my trailer, shirtless, in rainbow suspenders and hoop pants, thinking how there's nothing funny about polyester in sweltering jungle heat.

All week the temperature's been brutal: ninety or worse, humidity like you wouldn't believe. Today's no better, but it's a travel day, thank God, except we're not moving. Rocky has the whole caravan squeezed into a shady rest stop just inside Connecticut. I can't pull any air into my trailer. I'm pacing, dripping sweat, thinking about how I'm wasting my life, honking my nose and making balloon animals for barely more than minimum wage.

Technically it's my day off, but I'm in makeup because we've got a mall promo up the road. No way to call in sick, though I am genuinely nauseous because I can't get any air. I'm no good in this kind of heat.

All month we've been touring New England, setting up Wednesdays around midnight, tearing down Mondays before dawn. Doing all these dinky little towns named after Native Americans, places I never heard of. Not our standard route, Rocky admits. And for once he's not lying, because I checked with Lester, our egg-headed strongman, and Lester tells me it's true. We're skipping all of last year's dead spots, doing the money towns, those sweet honey pots thick with baby boomers and lots of small churches.

Lester is a former CPA, and his assessment isn't at all reassuring. His roughed out figures (using conservative estimates) show Rocky's Circle Circus to be hurting, and hurting bad. According to Lester, Rocky's cash flow is running slower than a dying man's morphine drip.

So I'm smoking dope and pacing, worrying about my future. I've got a bad case of the jitters, though I'm not seriously concerned because logic dictates you don't fire your last clown, no matter how bad the numbers get. Nevertheless, I keep waiting for something bad to happen, for the other big floppy shoe to drop: for my ex-wife's lawyers to track me down, or the state police to haul all our asses off to jail, or for one of the tigers to throw a hissy fit and rip open my jugular.

All summer our two big cats, God bless 'em, have endured the jungle heat, which genetically at least they're used to, though most of the other animals look like they need a priest. The only really good news is that the climate is helping the gate, pulling people out of their hot little houses. The snack bar is setting records; between shows, Rocky has us all taking turns running for ice.

I'm doing eight performances a day—five with the tigers, three with the Martinez brothers (a pair of convicted felons with moustaches the size of coat hangers, and not really brothers—merely second cousins who share an unnatural interest in playing with fire). Between shows I'm getting a lousy thirty-minute break, during which I'm supposed to eat, shit, repaint my face, and then make balloon animals for anything under four feet. Except it's too hot to move. And the last thing I need in this heat is an ex-felon juggling a flaming torch past my ear. But when Rocky says work, we work.

I've got my trailer's porthole-sized window wedged open, but the place is still like a pizza oven. I'm studying the pinkish stain my wig left on my pillowcase, when the boss man himself starts pounding on my door, crashing his fists like thunder, making the walls shake. In a voice deeper than God's, he reminds me that we've got a two-hour promo in a mall parking lot two miles up the road. "Quick gig. No elephants, no torches, no Martinez Brothers. Just you and the tigers showing your teeth."

Twenty minutes later, we're moving again. We circle back to the interstate, clog the middle lane, all our trailers and trucks tailgating one another. I don't have a valid driver's license, so the kid who works the Dunk Tank is my designated driver. I'm rocking side to side while wrestling with my racquet-sized shoes, wishing I'd taken a dump in the woods when I had the chance, when through the front window I observe Rocky's truck veering toward an exit.

"Hey! Follow him," I shout to the kid. "Follow the tigers."

But the dumb jerk's up there with his Sony headphones capping his ears, oblivious to the real world. So with one shoe on I lurch forward and bang on the glass. He's numb, and despite his forty-dollar investment I can hear the crappy music leaking out of his head.

I kick the wall between us. I thump and bang until I get his attention, then I give him the thumbs right. He blinks and nods, his mouth spreading into a jack-o'-lantern grin that would scare the Madonna.

I know a fuck-you grin when I see one, so I squash my rubber nose up against the glass. "Eyes on the road, asshole!"

He jerks us into the exit lane. I watch until I can read the lettering on the back of Rocky's truck, then I sit on the floor and straighten my laces. I need to look sharp. Today, it's just the boss man, the tigers, and me.

It's a laugh shot, really. A swindle aimed at the helpless parents of spoiled youngsters. Entice the little ones with the clown and pull in the whole family is the scheme. So with Simba and Rambo posing on their platforms, I hand out yellow tickets through the bars, free passes good for brats twelve and under. I give 'em away by the handfuls, because they're worthless and the sooner I get done, the better. I slip extras to the pretty moms and the pathetically old, keeping my white-gloved hands well out of reach of the teenagers.

On a dare, or a whim, a maladjusted teen will snatch your gloves and run off like a spooked monkey. Sometimes they go for the wig, pulling at a thread not meant to be pulled. The worst of them, the truly angry kids, will turn the worthless passes into ammunition. So I avoid as many teenagers as I can, handing them nothing, because spit balls and other paper projectiles are a hazard when working with tigers. The older kids think it's all a game, like I'm a cartoon, like the tigers don't have real teeth.

Last month in Schenectady, before this miserable heat swept in, Simba caught a paper glider dead-center in her good eye. Poor baby nearly ripped my arm off.

My wound stretched shoulder to elbow, though it wasn't as painful as it later looked or should have been. Once I got past the shock of it, I hammed it up, high-stepping as I ran around the cage, all the while applying pressure, squeezing like a son of a bitch to stop the hemorrhage. Once I got Simba calmed down, I gave her a wet kiss right on the snout. She's half-blind, the poor thing, but she knows my smell. Then I crumbled the paper glider and put it in my mouth.

The Schenectady crowd went gaga. The fools thought it was just part of the show. They hooted and hollered, loving every minute.

Backstage, Rocky's wife, Ruthie, stitched the wound with a needle and thread. "This will definitely scar," she said, shaking her head at me.

"Sew, baby, sew," I said, smearing white-face on the bloody towel she'd fixed into a tourniquet.

She worked with such precision and skill that I wanted to watch every movement, but I simply couldn't. Instead, I bit down against the pain and admired the heart-shaped sweat stain on Ruthie's blouse. I was about ready to faint when Rocky stuck his head in to remind me, of all things, that I'm only a few weeks away from complete health benefits.

Ruthie told him to shut up. "Something this deep requires a surgeon."

Rocky and I grinned at one another, but we got caught.

"I'm talking Frankenstein scar," Ruthie said. "Are either one of you registering that?"

Rocky rubbed his arm in the exact spot where Simba had cut mine to the bone.

"Hey, as long as it's not the face," I said, which is my basic philosophy on life.

"Hold still," Ruthie said, making me wince.

Though she's no beauty queen, on a chilly night with a beer buzz and a hard-on, I could definitely go for Ruthie. She's headstrong, with a brain between her ears, and generally that's a hands-down no-boner for me, because I'm hypo-allergic to educated women. But if Rocky weren't around, say, if he had a massive coronary, I'd definitely take aim at getting Ruthie's cute ballerina torso butt-naked and belly-down. And I'd wager she wouldn't put up too much of a struggle.

Our stop in Providence is poorly planned. We've had no TV time, only a couple of radio spots and a small chintzy ad in the Sunday paper. The mob in the mall parking lot is substandard. Barely enough people to fill a school bus, and most of them are teenagers. But I whoop it up just the same, hopping around in the heat like I've been huffing polyurethane.

When all the tickets are disbursed, I wobble my knees like I'm so shocked and disappointed to be out of tickets that I'm going to drop dead between the tigers. Then I fall into a reverse-flip one-handed handstand, balancing on my good arm, holding my position until the crowd breaks into mild unenthusiastic applause.

Once I've got them smiling, I scuffle with the tigers, wink at the babes, twist a couple of dozen balloon animals for the kiddies, and occasionally squirt my flower through the bars at some teenager. From time to time, I turn a few heads by throwing my voice deep into the crowd. "Bravo," I say. And: "This guy's good!" And: "I'm taking the whole family to see this clown!"

At first no one knows it's me, then some punk catches on.

"It's the clown talking," he says. "Watch his throat."

What this pimply mallrat doesn't know, of course, is that ventriloquism comes from the Latin, meaning, literally, to speak from the belly. Everybody always thinks it's done in the throat, but the belly is where the air comes from. The trick is pushing the right amount of air past your vocal cords, using your stomach muscles to squeeze up the little puffs and whispers. For a while, I fake like the tigers are talking, first Rambo, who's got a metastasized cancer running all through him, then Simba, who's clawing her ass like she's spawning fleas again. I project two or three taunts at a couple of tall black kids, one of them a wiry scarecrow palming a basketball; the other, a beefy giant wearing his hat backwards. The kid with the ball strikes a Statue of Liberty pose and shoots me a look like he personally wants to bite my head off. I counter by tickling Simba's throat. When she stretches her mouth I pinch her fangs while pumping a scratchy growl up from my stomach. She roars and I roar, and Rambo, not to be outdone, throws in a pathetic little growl of his own. The whole front row retreats a step and a couple of brats in strollers scream like it's the Apocalypse.

Afterwards, minus my nose and wig, I smoke a pin-joint of primo Hawaiian in my trailer. The dope is courtesy of Lester, a sample of the batch he's trying to sell. I blow a stream of smoke at the window and watch the crowd scatter. My makeup pinches every pore, and my armpits are itching. (Heat rash? Fleas?) But all I want to do now is get high and forget I'm a clown.

When the tarpaulin drops on the tiger's cage, the last few stragglers slink away. Yellow tickets are scattered everywhere; they cover the asphalt like water lilies dead from the heat. A few yards in front of me, a couple of chic moms with strollers linger, gabbing to one another and sucking up the sun.

One holds a cigarette scissored between her long fingers. I check her out. She's sharp—a Scandinavian blonde with hair cropped like a Nazi helmet. She's wearing a yellow tank top several sizes too small, stone-washed cut-offs, rope sandals. A real looker. I remember her coming up to the cage and putting her hand out, her inch-long fingernails, pink as cotton candy, reaching toward me like claws. (I handed her a stack of passes so thick that had they been U.S. currency, she could have retired.)

I crouch close to the window, touch my nose to the glass, make a little clicking sound in my throat, and immediately sense a stiffness forming somewhere down in my floppy pants. I think about rapping the glass and inviting both ladies in.

Cigar, anyone?

Slouching beside Blondie, another mother, wild red hair tucked and tied off with a white ribbon, produces a thick stack of photos from her straw handbag. She's cute, too, with a broad European nose and a jaw line that suggests at least one Neanderthal shanghaied some *Homo sapiens* bride. Red looks delicious in her striped running shorts and V-necked T-shirt. But she's yesterday's coffee compared with Blondie, who is absolutely drop-dead bury-me-with-a-hard-on gorgeous. Heart-shaped ass. Bullet breasts. Big doll eyes. She's a full-lipped, animated talker. Even her teeth are sexy. Richly tanned arms and legs, slender and smooth.

She's tall, nervous, and thin. While she gabs she pinches her hips, lifts her chin, squares her shoulders, shakes her hair. Did I mention her long nails remind me of cotton candy?

Rocky used to have a cotton candy machine, an ancient monster with a crank-up awning. Some nights Lester and I would get that monster spinning, and we'd whip up a batch—we'd go crazy mixing colors. The bearings were bad and the thing made a racket, so we couldn't run it long. We'd pull the spun sugar out with our bare hands and feed ourselves like monkeys.

I could eat Blondie's hair like that—a sweet cottony handful at a time, taking pause to lick between my fingers.

Her teeth glint in the sun as the sweet smoke develops into a nice warm buzz. I put the joint to my lips, but it's dead. I fish out a cigarette, the last in the pack. It's slightly bent but smokable. I light up and practice my French inhale while I watch Blondie steer her stroller toward the mall, her ass doing a cha-cha. A real high-stepper.

When she stops to let a Porsche back out of a space, I watch the driver give her an assessing look, then peel out, tires screeching. She starts again, unfazed: a two-handed push to get going, then settles into a one-handed rumba rhythm ain't-I-adorable glide. I mock-punch the lump in my pants, saying, "Down, Simba. Down, Boy!"

Let me tell you how it is: Once in a blue moon, pig-faced Priscilla, who can ride a pony one-handed through a fiery hoop, will visit my trailer and we'll play hide the weenie until one of us gets bored or tired, but other than that, clown life ain't no bed of concubines. Tugging at my waistband, I shout at my dick to please remember that it and I are sworn to a sacred oath. Forget Rocky's rules on fraternizing, I'm talking my face is painted on an egg shell hanging in the Clown Hall of Fame. I'm fully registered, and that makes blacklisting me easier than filling pie tins with whipped cream. I peel off my costume and put everything on hangers. I scrub up real good, then squeeze into jeans and a fishnet sweater, no shirt. I grab my wallet and tuck it into a side pocket where it makes a little square. From my dressing table, I take out this flip phone

23

with a dead battery and shove it into my back pocket. Then I go outside to find Rocky. He's up front, checking the tarpaulin around the tiger cage, pulling on knots. The back of his shirt is soaked with sweat.

It's hot. Rocky is chewing an unlit cigar. He is short and heavyset. He works smoothly, like a prizefighter rehearsing in slow motion. His bald head is too small for his neck and chest, and he reminds me a little of Curly from the original Three Stooges, only sunburnt and a little less round. When he glimpses me out of the corner of his eye, he works his cigar and looks across the lot. Free passes are littered everywhere.

Rocky squints at the sun and says, "Do me a favor, okay?"

"What's that, boss?"

"Don't alienate the customers, okay? Not before they've become customers, okay? And don't make the little kids cry. It's not on our program."

"Gotcha, boss."

Behind the tarpaulin, the tigers are padding back and forth, antsy in the heat. Rocky wipes his hands on the front of his shirt as he comes over. The shirt has a picture of Simba and Rambo with their heads together beneath the words *Circle Circus, Inc.* Simba is showing teeth, but Rambo, who's dying, looks bored.

Rocky slides a hand over his scalp like he's smoothing hair. He looks me up and down. "You quitting today?"

It's our little joke, because I'm the third clown in eighteen months. And because I've never worked with animals before.

"Yeah, I'm running off to join civilization."

He snorts. "That's funny," he says. He squints toward the mall. The cars in between appear to be wavering in the unbearable heat. After a three count, he wags his head. "Something you need in there?"

"Running in for smokes. If that's alright?"

He checks the glitzy watch strapped upside down to his fat wrist. "Don't be long. We're out of here in twenty."

I crank up the wattage on my smile. I imagine screwing his wife while he's dangling from a meat hook. "Yes, sir. Twenty minutes. Gotcha, chief."

He taps his watch. "Twenty means twenty." He gives me a stern look.

"No problem," I say, shuffling a few steps toward the mall, making a point to stomp on the littered tickets like I'm stepping stones across a swamp. One adheres to my sneaker and travels with me a few steps until

I shake it off. A dozen car-widths away, Rocky shouts, "Hey, clown, how's that paper cut?"

I don't turn, so he can't see me smile. "You want to see the scar."

"What scar? My wife sews as straight a line as anybody."

When I turn to see if he's smiling, he's bent over, scooping up tickets faster than a migrant worker harvesting potatoes.

The mall's AC feels good on my face. It feels wonderful for about three seconds. Then I'm suddenly chilled to the bone. Frigid air is coming at me from six directions. I rub my hands together as I walk. The mall's center is an oasis—all ferns and dark glimmering wood in a sunken area with a pool-sized fountain surrounded by stone benches. Blondie is sitting on one, legs crossed, rocking her stroller. I circle round to get a better angle. She's got her chin propped on a hand supported by an elbow supported by a knee. She taps her foot, mechanically, like someone upstairs is working her strings. She drums her long fingernails against her cheek, starring at the slippery tiles. I can't figure if she's talking to herself, or to the baby.

I ride the escalator to the second level and get a sniper's view. Down in the middle of the little oasis, it's just her and the kid, who is slumped left, passed out cold. I think about what a woman who looks like that says when she talks to herself. If I looked like that I'd speak only to the mirror and snub everything else. I'd be like that queen in *Snow White* who was all in a tizzy when the mirror said she wasn't top banana.

I start to get hard looking down at Blondie's leg jerking and twitching like it's on a string. She doesn't look like she's going any place fast, so I duck into CVS to get cigarettes.

While I'm in line, standing behind a blue-haired woman cradling enough deodorant to slick down a football team, I try on sunglasses. There's a tiny mirror mounted on the carousel display. I look at myself at angles and think: a young Jerry Lewis with a John Lennon haircut. I like what I see, so I wear the glasses up to the register. When the teenage clerk looks at me, I snap off the tag and hand it to her. She shows me her braces, then seals her mouth with a professional cashier's smile. I get a pack of Marlboros, too. I tell her I don't need a bag. She hands me my change with the receipt, her eyes already focused on the next poor soul.

At the railing, I think it's the sunglasses playing tricks with the light, but no, Blondie is on the move, all right. With renewed vigor, she's steering a collision course for JCPenney. Fifty feet up, I stroll in the same direction, sliding the pack of Marlboros along the railing, while watching Blondie's butt bounce past a pushcart of sports memorabilia. I'm figuring, okay, JCPenney, anchor store, must have a second level. When she disappears beneath a banner that reads, "Wacky Wednesday is Discount Madness," I pick up my pace.

I find the store's entrance and cut though Ladies' wear, admiring the tight sweaters on the headless mannequins along the way. I ride the escalator down, walking a few steps ahead of the glide until I spot her; then I backpedal upward until I get my bearings. She's in Housewares, admiring a tire-sized skillet.

I stand in Jewelry, behind a young couple holding hands, but I don't take my eyes off Blondie. When she starts toward the exit, I follow. I'm less than ten feet behind her when a woman in a polka-dot dress crosses my path and takes up a position there. She's a sales clerk, with a name plate centered between her breasts that reads: Dotty. As I sidestep, Dotty asks if I'd like to open a JCPenney account.

"New customers receive an additional ten percent off all purchases for thirty days."

"Not today, Dotty," I say, brushing past her.

Twenty feet ahead, Blondie punches the button for the elevator. I stand directly behind her, admiring her bottom half.

"Pardon me," I say, "I'm doing a survey for the Monks of Mercy. By any chance, are you an unwed mother?"

She tosses her hair like she's doing a shampoo commercial, blinks.

"No, I'm not," she says. "Why?"

I look at the kid, a dirty-faced blob, sleeping and sucking air. I smile at the gold band on Blondie's ring finger. "Separated or divorced?"

She nods no, looks at the child. When she looks at me again, her eyes flicker.

I touch my chin, puckering like I'm a wizard pondering a spell. "A widow, perhaps?"

Her eyes narrow as she takes a step back. Her sweet mouth curls up and breaks into a dubious smile. "Who are you?" she says.

One other time, at the grand opening of a mall outside Georgia, I screwed a woman in her car in broad daylight. We were parked beside a dumpster near the customer pickup of a toy store. The woman, a chrome blonde with the hard body of an athlete, not your typical weak-kneed Georgian peach, believed I was a security guard. She actually believed her car was illegally parked in a handicapped zone.

I lean closer. "Mall security, ma'am."

But it's no use—I can't keep a straight face. I'm too high or too nervous. For a few hazy seconds, I get lost in her liquid eyes. Then I start rambling: "We've just been alerted that a battalion of terrorists are converging on the premises. They're armed with exploding babies and are apparently hell-bent on ruining a perfectly good shopping day." I nod at the kid who's dripping drool onto a pale blue shirt that reads *Grandpa's Pride & Joy*. "I'm afraid I'll have to check the little tyke's diaper, ma'am, just to be safe."

"Wait a second," she says, poking my arm with a pink fingernail. "You were that clown. I recognize the voice."

Which is preposterous, really, because one voice is not the other.

"Clown, ma'am?" My left leg trembles, going crazy as I take out the flip phone and snap it open like I'm Kirk signaling the Enterprise. "What clown is that, ma'am?"

"The one outside, before. In the cage. You gave me all those tickets." She tosses her hair again. Her smile bubbles and collapses. "Is this a gag?" she says.

I smile, not missing a beat. "Not so loud," I say. "And please! Don't look directly at the camera." Hitching a thumb over my shoulder, I drop my voice to a cool whisper. "Not yet, anyway. Freddie isn't quite ready for us."

She looks past me. "Freddie?" she says. Her face does a series of lifts and folds. "Oh my God," she says.

I mouth into the flip phone. "Tight zoom, Fred. This is our girl. Get ready for a take."

Then, tight-lipped, nostrils flared, I imitate electrical popping sounds and a crackly voice that answers, "Roger on that. Over."

Blondie stares at the flip phone. "I knew it," she says.

She looks down at her sleeping baby, smiles, touches her mouth, looks off. Her shoulders shudder and shake. One knee buckles slightly and she puts a hand on my chest. Steadying herself, she gives me half a smile, delicious and pink. "You scared me," she says, but her eyes, all wet and shining, say something else.

"Don't be nervous," I say. "Turn and smile." I loop an arm around her shoulder, pulling her in, nudging her left. We stand hip to hip. She's beaming. People stop to stare.

"I can't see," she says, squinting.

"You're not supposed to. Look straight ahead." I clamp the dead phone under my chin, cramping my neck. "Ready, Fred?"

Constricting my throat, I squeeze out more static. In a voice that sounds like it's underwater, I reply, "Ready when you are."

More bewildered shoppers gather round, stirring like wasps at a picnic. "They're filming a commercial," someone says. There's a chorus of oohs and ahhs. So I take off my glasses, grin at the crowd. "This will only take a moment, folks." I give Blondie a squeeze, aligning my fingers with her ribs. I place my other hand beneath her chin, steering her gaze to a spot no one else can see. "Right there," I say. "Big smile."

A few people squeeze behind us, mugging for the camera that isn't there.

"What channel will this be on?" somebody says.

Blondie repeats the question into my ear, her tone very much like a shy starlet on the set of her first major film. Her sweet voice vibrates all though me, until she adds, "You know, so I can tell my husband."

This revelation doesn't impact as much as it should because I'm watching two men in Catholic school blazers, both carrying walkie-talkies, racing down the escalator.

"All times," I say. "It's a multichannel package."

Blondie moves her mouth as if to ask something new, but I cut her off. I press a finger to her lips.

"Okay, people," I say. "Gather 'round, folks. Let's get this right the first time. Together, on three. Circle Circus is coming to Providence!" Their dumb looks are encouraging. "Everybody ready? All together ..."

As I count off, I smooth my hand up and over Blondie's ribs and give the underside of her boob a careful squeeze. Maybe she notices, maybe she doesn't. If she's so freaking happy, why isn't she home baking cookies and knitting a Christmas scarf? Why is she lollygagging at the mall, posing for fake commercials with every clown she meets? On three, everyone shouts so loud we rouse the baby. The little creature's face tightens, then expands as he unleashes a scream like a wounded monkey. Blondie pulls away and scoops the brat up, cooing and cuddling. She looks at me as if for help, then lifts its little hand and flaps a wave for the faraway camera. I grin at the security guards, one a tall Stan Laurel type, the other a square-headed buffoon with a build like Hercules. I kiss the baby on the forehead, then, tilting in farther, give Mamma a hard kiss right on the mouth. I try slipping my tongue in but she jerks away, her face suddenly pink as her fingernails. Her eyes roll, then narrow, and for half a second she looks like she's deliberating the quality of the air, deciding if it's safe to breathe. Her nostrils flare. One shoulder dips as her legs start to go.

"Somebody, please, take my baby."

She sways; both knees buckle. Some fat lady with a bad wig grabs the kid just as Blondie teeters into the arms of Hercules.

As I'm backing away, Blondie unleashes a series of short piercing screeches that could pass for B-movie scream-queen impressions, as a chorus of beefy male voices shout in my direction. I get my elbows rocking and start speed-walking like my pants are on fire. Because it's all about an exit now, all about finding a door. I push through one, then another. The heat hits me like a wall. At the far end of the lot, littered tickets are everywhere, but the landscape has changed dramatically—no truck, no trailer. Rocky's packed up and gone.

Behind me, it's all business, all footsteps and voices, a regular stampede of crazies. And just like that time in Schenectady when Simba went a little nuts, I'm center stage, all eyes upon me, and my only concern is getting out alive.

All Set for Ardor?

The place I want to tell you about, this old building at the west end of Main Street—it's a strip joint now. My father goes there two or three times a week and insists it's a "clean, well-lighted, establishment" run by "top notch professional people." He refers to it as his Gentleman's club. Which is rich. You'll see how rich that statement is. Just give me a minute.

The look hasn't changed much on the outside. Still a low, squat structure, all stucco and white, though a new, smaller sign flashes where the old neon used to buzz and hum. In the side alley they've added an adult bookstore, a sort of gift shop where you can buy videos (and used clothing) of the dancers. My father calls them Lady Entertainers. He owns a couple of tapes and has boasted long distance that several of the women are local talent—girls I went to school with, and whom, he tells me, I could have dated if I had "possessed half a backbone as a boy."

On a number of my visits home, I've driven by, either to pick the old man up or to drop him off. A few times he's invited me in, once as adamantly as if he owned the place, and another time, viscous and drunk, clutching my shirt, begging me to join him for "one god damn lousy drink," then weeping and moaning, as if he knew the real reason for my refusal.

You couldn't pay me to go in there, not for an ice cold beer on the hottest day of the year. And not because of what its become, either. Since my own divorce I've been to my share of clubs, Gentleman and otherwise, and have had that one beer too many then drooled like a fool and spent more than I should. And personally I hold no ill-feelings against naked woman, or the men who get a thrill slipping fan-folded currency into G-strings. I'm not against good old fashioned lust as long as it's kept in check. No, I won't go in because of what the place used to be.

Years ago, before the whole downtown went to hell, that exact spot housed a Chinese restaurant called Lucky Luke's. Among its distinctions was a marquee like a movie theater, valet parking, deep padded horseshoe booths, and a huge one-page menu the approximate size of a major league strike zone.

If I close my eyes, I can still see that menu, a poster-sized memory tacked into a small dark corner of my childhood. From about the time I could read, this giant menu filled me with awe. The scrolling fire-breathing dragons aside, there wasn't a single price beside a single item,

---

30

or any hint that money was involved. Even then I knew a thing or two about money. I knew we didn't have any. I knew Lucky Luke's wasn't meant for people like us. Never-the-less, once a year my mother took me there for my birthday. Just the two of us.

I didn't like Chinese food any more than my father, who year after year preferred to babysit my sister rather than come along, but I did enjoy my mother's company immensely, and with the approach of each age relished the idea of having her full attention for a few hours. Just the two of us.

After dinner we'd take the long way home, strolling past houses we could never own, working our way down past the old mills, then back across the river, to celebrate with horribly sweet cake; and then I'd get to open my two or three presents, typically some cheap plastic toy I didn't want, and some item of clothing I just happened to need. So in a sense I considered these private dinners—our annual date, my mother called it—the very best gift of all.

Usually I'd order the half-broiled chicken—listed under the small American Foods section of the menu—while my mother dined on a variety of exotic dishes, some of which arrived at our table still flaming. She'd always pay cash, taking money from a small book of envelopes with a red vinyl cover on which was printed BUDGET. I never got more than an upside down glance at the actual bill, and the one time I did the numbers only proved to make me dizzy.

Year after year my father grumbled at the unnecessary expense, saying we could eat for a week on what she'd be putting out for one nights worth of "cat guts and noodles"; but my mother argued Luke's was the very best restaurant in town, and the only truly decent place within walking distance suitable for a proper birthday celebration.

If he tried to bully her, she pointed out that these private dinners had become a tradition. When called upon, I backed her one hundred percent. Even after I understood the dent this once a year extravaganza put in the family budget, I took her side, saying it was me who wanted to go. I knew firsthand the thrill she got from eating at Luke's. I'd seen the shine in her eyes when the Chinese waiters, dressed in black silk pajamas, fussed over us like we were royalty. She adored how polite and soft-spoken they remained even when you couldn't understand a word they were saying.

Mo warder, miss? Sum ting elks, miss? Howdah boy leek is chicken, miss? I ba-wing you for chun cookie, okey doe?

31

My mother cleaned other people's houses for a living and sometimes had to assist at dinner parties and snotty little get-togethers; she'd have to dress up in a black house dress and a frilly white apron and walk around all night in four-inch heels carrying a tray of foods she couldn't identify. Lucky Luke's charged an arm and a leg for a breast and a wing, but sitting in their horseshoe shaped booths, with a frilly paper lantern overhead, a dozen willing waiters no more than a finger-snap away, made her, I believe, feel as wealthy and powerful as the people she scrubbed toilets for. Sometimes she'd point out a group of people and whisper, that's Mrs. So-and-so, her husband owns the supermarket, or, There's Mr. What's-his-face. His company built the dry cleaners where your father worked, and they're putting up that new donut shop beside it.

If somebody she recognized looked our way, she'd give a snappy little wave, and nod her chin while stretching her mouth into a tight smile. I can't remember anyone ever waving back, and on a couple of occasions I pointed this out to her. She'd then insist, quite vehemently, that so-and-so had indeed made some sign of recognition, but that I'd merely missed it. I was usually up to my eye balls behind the huge menu, squinting at a dragon, guessing at the contents of, say, Egg-drop soup, so I never doubted her for a moment.

My mother, you see, wasn't hard to look at. Tall and slender (what my father called "leggy") and with the delicate doll-like features of a ballerina, she was exactly the kind of woman most men stretched their necks to get a second glimpse of.

The night I want to tell you about, the night of my thirteenth birthday, someone not only spotted my mother but came over to our booth and slid in beside her. The man's name was Frank Zorn and I later learned he was a big shot lawyer with a wife and two kids of his own. He sat down and smiled at my mother as if he had just returned from the men's room and we'd been holding our breaths, and our orders, until his anticipated return. He was about the same age and build as my father, though much better looking, with more hair, and wearing red suspenders over an open collared flowery shirt. He held a ceramic pineapple from which a tiny pink umbrella sprouted, pitching and rolling in whatever fluid was contained therein.

"Emperor Qianglong couldn't get waited on tonight," he said, addressing the room at large.

From behind my menu, I watched my mother slide over a little. Her face was flush red, and her eyes were scanning the room. She shuddered a breath, then placed her folded hands on the table's edge as if she were praying. She didn't say a word.

"So, what've we got here," Frank said, eyeing me over the top of his pineapple.

My mother cleared her throat. "This ... is my son," she said weakly. "We're celebrating his birthday." She closed her eyes, seemingly exhausted from this tiny speech. "Say hello to Frank, Marty."

"Hello Frank," I said.

Frank instantly sat up, thrusting his shoulders against the high cushioned seat. His face took on an expression I can only describe as outright shock at my ability to speak.

"Well, now," he said. "Isn't he the polite little guy." He set down his pineapple and reached across the table. Before I knew what he was doing he'd seized my right hand in both of his. He held it as if it were a dead sparrow that had just crashed head-first into the table top. I looked at my mother for help. Frank's fingers were ice cold and somewhat clammy, but beyond that I was generally opposed to hand-holding, period, particularly with a man.

My mother sighed heavily. She couldn't have looked more bewildered if Frank had brought out a meat cleaver, chopped off my hand at the wrist, and begun to eat it in front of her. Fearing something along those lines, I pulled back, a blundering move on my part, because Frank mistook my second, more forceful tug, as an invitation to arm wrestle. He tightened his grip and effortlessly brought my hand closer. I felt the seat of my pants lift and the table's edge cut into my belly. He might have succeeded in pulling me out of the booth entirely, if a smiling waiter hadn't appeared.

"All set for ardor?" Frank released his hold on me and I flopped into my seat. He showed the waiter his pineapple.

"Yea. Another shanghai," Then he smiled at my mother, who, at the waiter's appearance, had picked up her menu and was using it to fan herself.

"You want a shanghai, babycakes?" Frank said.

She shook her head. It was more of a tremor, really. The "babycakes" had startled me and I examined her face for some reaction. Once, at a bus stop, a man who'd been ogling her legs, had called her "sweet stuff" and she'd threatened to take his eye out with her umbrella. I couldn't believe she was letting Frank get away with "babycakes."

"You want to ardor food now," the waiter said.

"No," my mother said, finding her voice. "Not just yet, thank you."

The waiter smiled, then bowed, then moved off. I watched him stop at another booth and launch, whole-heartedly, into a similar routine. When I looked at Frank, he was thumbing through a folded stack of crisp currency. The outermost bill was a hundred and my eyes shot open. I held my breath as he flipped past a number of fifties, pulled a twenty from the middle, and tossed it nonchalantly across the table.

"Hey Marky boy. How 'bout doing me a tremendous favor and getting me change for that."

I looked at my mother who was pinching the bridge of her nose. Her cheeks had drained from red to white. I waited for her to explain that my name wasn't Marky boy, or Marky anything, but Marty, more preferably Martin, plain and simple. Her own name was Rose and she'd bite your ear off if you stretched it to Rosy.

"So whadaya say," Frank said. "Can you do that for me?" His left hand disappeared beneath the table.

I watched her focus on the paper lantern suspended above our booth. There was a snaky red dragon, shaped like an S. It was diffused by the light, slightly pinkish, but it was the same dragon from the doors and the menu. She was staring at it as though she'd never seen a dragon before.

"Yo!" Frank said. "Earth to Marky. Come in, Marky."

"My name is Marty," I said through clenched teeth. I didn't take my eyes off my mother. If anyone was in orbit, she was, and I'd firmly decided I wasn't running any errands until she gave the okay.

"Didn't I say Marty," Frank asked. "What did I say?"

I was about to tell Frankie Boy what he'd said, when my mother picked up the twenty and handed it to me. "Go on," she said, blinking. "See if they've got change."

At that moment a scream of laughter erupted from the booth behind us and I stretched my neck to look. I glimpsed a woman in a tight silvery dress that appeared to be made of metal squares raise a stemmed glass high over her head. "To Custer," she said, "and to the savage bastards that cut his hair!"

Frank said, "So, how 'bout we take a little walk. Just you and me. I want to show you my new car. Va-room, va-room."

My mother leaned into him just as I whipped my head around. She replied something I couldn't hear above the howling group behind us, but Frank's face revealed an obvious refusal to his invitation. "Come on," he said, pleading. "Ten minutes. Then I'll buy you and the kid dinner."

She was looking straight ahead—not at me, not at the group behind us, but at something or someone far across the room. Frank raised his pineapple. He smiled at me, as though suddenly realizing I hadn't left.

"You don't mind if I borrow your mother for ten minutes, do you, son?"

It was a face-freezing question. I felt my jaw lock up as I quietly slid out of the booth. I couldn't have answered if I'd wanted to.

As I zigzagged through the maze of clustered booths, making my way toward the register, I glanced back once. I wasn't tall enough to get a clean look but I'm almost certain Frankie boy had an arm around her. It was the unsettling after-the-fact type of certitude that makes one wish they'd been born blind.

At the register a stunning Asian woman asked me how I wanted my change. She had straight black hair that fell past her hips, and for a dozen or so heartbeats I was honestly more concerned with her huge eyes and prominent white teeth than with the breakdown of Frankie boy's twenty. When she asked a second time, I stammered, "Quarters, please."

"Oil quotas?" she said.

I nodded at a butterfly curved around her breast.

She handed over two orange rolls. I clenched one in each fist, and as I made my way back, I worked my arms like I was flexing dumb bells.

When I saw my mother alone in the booth, with Frank nowhere in sight, I stopped pumping the quarters and picked up my pace a step. I took a short cut between two identical waiters talking gibberish beside a small rocky island of fake greenery. The area was divided by a narrow stream of running water, with wavering blue lights beneath, to give the effect, I assumed, of the ocean. As I stepped across, I hoped we'd seen the last of Frankie boy. I slid into the booth, put the quarter rolls on the table, and immediately realized we hadn't. He'd most certainly be back for his change. I frowned at my mother, who angled her menu to shield herself from my accusing eyes.

"So where's what's his face," I said.

"Excuse me," she said, in a voice shaky and weak.

"The asshole," I said.

She slapped her menu down, and thrust her face forward. "Watch your mouth, Marty. For god's sake, remember where we are."

35

She looked like she was deliberating wiping the look off my face, and suddenly I thought of my father, at home, eating tuna from a can, and feeding Cheerios to my sister while we sat in a fancy restaurant where no one spoke English. "Who is that guy," I said.

"Lower your voice, please." She picked up her menu again. "It's not important who he is."

I fired a warning shot across her bow. "I bet dad doesn't know about him."

She lowered her menu halfway, revealing all but her chin, then dropped it to her lap. "That man," she said, "not that it's any of your business, is Frank Zorn, a very respected attorney, and a former selectman. He and I went to high school together. On occasion I see him at the parties I work at."

"Well, he forgot his money," I said, pushing the quarters at her. She stopped them from rolling off the table, then relocated them to the center. She straightened up a bit, looking wounded and hurt.

"For your information," she said, "he left that money for you. He told me to tell you happy birthday."

"I don't want his stupid money," I said, and rolled the quarters at her again.

She picked them both up and put them in her purse. "Fine," she said. "I'll keep them."

"Fine," I said.

"And the next time you want spending money, you can think about the twenty dollars in quarters you threw away."

I positioned my menu so I wouldn't have to look at her. I was afraid I might say something I'd be sorry for.

"All set for ardor now?"

I looked at the waiter. His perfect smile made me want to puke. What the hell were these people so god damn happy about, anyway?

"I'll have the mandarin duck," my mother said. "Chop suey, small. An order of egg rolls, and a bowl of won ton soup."

The waiter smiled and she handed him her menu. He put it under his arm and looked at me.

"I'm not hungry," I said and gave him my menu, too.

"What do you mean you're not hungry," my mother said. "Marty, it's your birthday dinner."

"I don't care. I'm not hungry," I said.

The waiter looked at my mother then at me. He held our menus as though we might want them back.

"Marty, why are you doing this?"

"What?" I said. "I'm not hungry."

"Marty, please don't be like that."

"Like what? I'm not hungry."

"Marty?"

The waiter said, "You wan mo time, miss? I give you mo time."

"Yes, please. Thank you," my mother said. She held her smile until he'd moved off.

"Marty, what's the matter," she said.

"Nothing," I said. "I want to go home."

"But why, Marty?"

"I feel sick. This place makes me sick, okay? I want to go. I don't want to eat here. I don't like the people here. I want to go home. Take me home," I said.

"All right, Marty. Okay. If that's what you want to do, that's what we'll do."

"It is," I said.

On our way to the door she pinched the sleeve of another waiter and told him to please cancel our order. "I'm very sorry," she said. He smiled politely, glanced over at our table, then bowed at my mother, as though the two rolls of quarters she'd left were meant for him.

Outside, on the sidewalk, she held my arm and I walked beside her for a while, matching her step for step. I kept my head down, my eyes on the sidewalk. I tried to step on every crack.

As we turned a corner she suddenly stopped and said, "There's still cake, you know." She smiled weakly. I stared at her unblinkingly, my eyes like slits, until her smile faded. As we crossed the street, she released her hold on my arm and without looking at me, she said, "Now when we get home, don't do anything stupid."

"Stupid like what?"

"Like shooting your mouth off about things you don't know about. Remember your father's blood pressure," she said.

I gave her what I hoped was a mean and vicious look—as powerful a look as I could manage in the days before I learned what love and marriage and heartache meant, before divorce taught me the pain of losing someone who'd vowed to love you forever. It was probably my most painful look to-date, and I'm sad to report my mother missed it entirely.

We walked the rest of the way in silence. I lagged several steps behind, watching the shine of her patent leather heels in the glare of street lights. Outside our building, when she stopped to fix her lipstick, I ran ahead. I bolted up the stairs as though running from a beast, leaving my mother a solid two flights behind admiring (or so I decided) her girlish reflection in a grease-fogged window. I pounded on our door until my father opened it. His hair was wet, wild looking, and he was holding a box of blue candles.

"What's happened," he said.

I watched his face.

"Where's your mother?" he said.

After an exchange of dead-eyed stares, I threw myself into his arms.

"Hey now," he said. "Hey birthday boy. What's all this?"

He smelled of tuna fish, Old Spice, and tobacco.

I held on to him and listened to the click-clacking of my mother's heels on the wooden stairs.

"What's wrong?" my father shouted. "The kid's shaking like a leaf. What in hell happened?"

I tried to answer before she did, before she soothed him with some calculated lie. I wanted to explain that the world had changed. Our world. His and mine. But I was sobbing uncontrollably, unable to catch my breath; and it was my mother who said, in a voice that echoed through our empty hall, "What can I tell you, Jack? The kid lost his taste for Chinese food."

That Whooshing Noise Before the End

The same Saturday I packed up all my stuff and moved out, I invited my wife to this French film about divorce. On the phone, she said, "You know this proves you're crazy, don't you?" And I didn't mind that remark because it had been a full six hours since I left her and she still sounded sober. But then she made me beg, and that wasn't pretty because I was at a payphone in the lobby of my new home, a rooming house on Providence's east side, and a couple of unsavory characters were waiting to use the phone. One was a wrinkly man, no more than a bag of old bones in a t-shirt and overalls, but the other was a bearded fellow, big as a bear, wearing a steel-gray Nazi-style motorcycle helmet, which is never a good sign. I nearly ran out of quarters before I convinced Lois to drive over and pick me up.

When she's not drinking, Lois is a practicing hotshot in her daddy's downtown Providence law firm. Mostly she handles Real Estate, closings and foreclosures, much of it over the phone while she gazes out a 16th story window. But she understood the legal side of separation inside and out. I wanted her to see what we were looking at on the everyday side. The movie review mentioned a contentious custody battle, something I hoped to avoid.

She showed up sober and late, then didn't speak ten words to me on the ride. When I asked about the children, how they were holding up, she tapped her watch. "We've been separated less than eight hours."

I told her that I'd quit smoking, though the truth was I had sneaked a few puffs that morning. She made a snorting sound, almost a laugh, and shook her head.

Then we hit traffic, due to a construction detour, and because of all the one-way streets we ended up parking half a mile away. I left my sweater on the seat of her Volvo, mainly because I didn't want to carry it, and that was a mistake because the theater was damp and cold, and the floor was sticky, and the seats were narrow, and the men's room smelled like a sewer.

The film was grainy and hard to follow. Fuzzy subtitles kept dancing along the screen. Thirty minutes into it, I stopped caring. I wanted a cigarette. I started praying for the projector to snag or for some fool to yell "Fire!"

Lois was antsy too, crossing and uncrossing her legs, repeatedly banging my elbow.

When the movie family sat down to dinner, I leaned in and pointed out the resemblance of their children to our own.

"I hate this movie," Lois said. "I'm going for a walk."

She stepped on my foot then shuffled out into the aisle, gripping her purse like a football. "If you're nice," she whispered, "I'll share what's in here."

She wiggled her eyebrows, but I already knew what she meant. For our tenth anniversary her father had given us an expensive silver flask, a heart-shaped thing, big as a human heart only thinner. Our names were on it, inscribed above the anniversary date. Full to the brim the thing held six ounces.

I watched Lois climb into the dark, then I hurried up the opposite aisle. I caught up with her by the lobby doors.

"Hey," I said, "When aren't I nice? I'm always nice. I'm too nice."

Lois was grinning beneath the EXIT sign. The people in the movie were yelling at one another in French.

The lobby was narrow as a barber shop and the refreshment stand seemed far too busy for the middle of a movie. While we stood in line, I asked Lois if the subtitles bothered her eyes.

She said, "I understand enough French to know that's not what they're saying."

Someone behind us said, "It's an Americanized version."

Lois rolled her eyes at me. She had her elbows extended outward to prevent anyone from cutting in front of us. She looked like a basketball player going for a rebound.

After I ordered, the girl fizzed soda to the brim. She spilled foam into the tray, tapped her foot, fizzed some more. She was around my daughter's age, and I instantly felt sorry for her. Her lips glowed glossy pink; her hair was cropped short as a boy's. She had a smile and a shape sure to make her popular, but her head definitely wasn't in the game.

I watched her slide the cup along the counter; her anxious eyes, outlined like a raccoon's, already on the next customer.

I wondered if her parents were divorced.

"Two fifty," she said.

"Is that all we get," Lois asked.

The girl directed a finger wave at someone who wasn't me.

"Ask her," Lois said, nudging my arm.

Lois was pretty, too. She looked sharp in suits and dresses, but casual clothes hung on her like curtains. On nights she didn't want to drink alone, she wore her nice outfits to bars where late working professionals go. Her friends called them lounges, but on the nights I had to fetch my wife from them, they looked like bars to me.

"Two-fifty," the girl said again, showing me her hand as though something were written there.

I felt Lois press against my arm. "Don't pay," she said.

The foam had settled and the cup was barely two-thirds full.

"I'd like to speak to the manager," Lois said.

"No she doesn't," I said.

"It's still two-fifty," the girl said.

I leaned on the glass and pointed to the cup with my chin.

"What's the deal," I said to the girl.

Her face went flat. "That's a small, okay? You ordered a small."

She glanced at Lois who was looking at me.

I said, "I know what I ordered. Where's the rest of it?"

The girl blinked like she was having a seizure. "We're out of small cups. That's a medium cup." She pointed above my head to three cups floating on a string. "It's the same thing, sir."

Lois banged her purse on the glass and started digging. She took out her wallet and her keys. I handed three dollars to the girl and she pushed the money into the register.

"Wait," Lois said. "I have two quarters."

"Now you have four," said the girl, handing Lois my change.

We sat through the rest of the film in the balcony, taking turns sipping from the flask and chasing it with soda. The movie made no sense. Words flashed faster than I could follow.

A full five minutes before the credits, the subtitles stopped completely. The music changed to a dull thumping drum solo. A split screen showed the woman in one country—France, I think—and the man, richly tanned, wearing ragged trousers and no shirt, emerging from a palm tree forest onto an endless white beach.

On the left the woman sat by a window overlooking a jagged skyline against a pasty sky; on the right the man gazed upon an emerald sea. It made no sense. All through the credits, they faced one another, smiling, while words rolled up between them.

Then the house lights came up, and people started filing out beneath us.

I smelled cigarette smoke. The stink seemed to be coming from every direction.

"Well, that was dumb," Lois said. "What the hell happened to the kids?"

She was loud, already slurring her words.

I swallowed what was left in the flask and stared at the screen.

"He's got them," I said. "They're safely hidden in the forest."

"That's crazy," Lois said. "They would have showed that."

"Poor bastard, he almost pulled it off, too." I handed Lois her silver heart. "Turns out her rich daddy's pockets were too deep and he was pals with all the judges." I tilted my head and directed what I hoped was a meaningful look. One of Lois's eyes seemed more open than the other.

I said, "That whooshing noise before the credits was a police chopper buzzing the bush."

"Ha. I think you're drunk," my wife said.

Oh, Alison!

1) Phil's Ghost

At our long-deceased stepfather's sixty-third birthday celebration mother serves us tomalley dip, presented on a rock crystal platter, the lumpy tomalley shaped like a dolphin; a sprig of parsley for the mouth, a sliver of pimento for an eye. In her heyday, before cancer zapped her strength, and even after that for a short time, Mom was the assistant chef in charge of a large kitchen staff at St. Joe's Hospital. Now, every post-burial birthday, she goes out of her way to whip up some dandy and exotic treat, her once-a-year effort to appease Phil's spiritual taste buds while simultaneously browbeating her adult children, Alison and me, who still make our living as lowly wait-persons.

"The Tomalley is for Phil," she says, spilling Ritz crackers into a ceramic seashell. "You two don't have to touch it."

At sixty-eight, arthritic, a nine-year survivor of colon cancer, with a full colostomy, and cataracts that make her officially and legally blind, she has outlived two husbands—the first a monster king, an abusive madman, the second a careful, gentle carpenter who built this country cottage with lumber he notched and pegged with his own two hands.

With her hair a silver white peach fuzz., her black prescription goggles in place, and a knotted chef's kerchief around her chicken-neck, she resembles a wrinkly ex-con who blowtorches bank vaults for a living.

Alison says, "What's that smell," and grimaces across the draped double-leafed table.

"Ma killed a dolphin," I tell her, and bite the side of my tongue.

I try not to stare at my sister when my mother is present. But today Alison looks stunning in her white dress, white stockings, a pair of Victorian ankle-high button-down pumps. A thin, vivid, dark eyed beauty.

The dining room, designed to be a bedroom, is boxy and cold, the dark-paneled walls crammed with framed photos. There are dozens of Alison and me. Alone. Together. Gawky grade school pictures, air-brushed studio portraits snapped at Sears, and other, more ancient parodies in antique oval frames: Alison with curls and ribbons; me with bow-ties and slicked back hair. In her high school yearbook shot my sister looks like Cindy Crawford without the mole. I stare at it for almost

---

a minute, then gaze around and feel my childhood breathing down my neck.

In the doorway my mother pretends to be a statue, her bulbous goggles reflecting two small images of me.

"What?" I say. "What did I do?"

She shifts her attention from me to the food.

To appease her, I fake at dipping a cracker, and stretching, place it into Alison's delicate mouth.

"Tell her it's good," I say.

My sister chews and pats her belly. "Um um good," she says.

For three seconds our mother plays at smiling, then abandons the effort. "Better taste good. God damn costs enough."

I lick cracker crumbs off my thumb. "Oh, that is good," I say. "You'll have to loan me the recipe."

"I'm not loaning you anything," she snarls.

"Is this from that Martha Stewart book we got you for your birthday?" Alison says, and gives me a sly wink.

Mother frowns. "Don't even mention that woman's name in my house." She makes a slight and unnecessary adjustment to the serving dish, then shuffles back toward her kitchen. The prep work for these celebrations exhausts her. For the next few days, she'll expect Alison to be at her beck and call.

All for Phil, dear dead Phil.

She steadies a blotchy claw-like hand on the door jamb and I think how it is some kind of miracle that she is able to navigate through this cluttered one-bedroom cottage (Phil's legacy, bought and paid for) without killing herself.

I want to shout, "The man is dead. For god's sake sit down and relax already."

2) Musical Chairs

Alison's theory is that mom has memorized furniture placement. "Move an end table in that shit shack and she'd be flat on her ass but pronto," she said on our ride over.

"Ha, ha," I said, chewing a thumbnail while I steered. Once a week Alison drives out to visit or chauffeur Mom to some medical building, but nearly two months have passed since I've last seen the old gal.

"We should take her out back and spin her around a couple of times. Leave her in that weed patch she calls a garden. See how she navigates from there."

"No," I said, "No, it's those damn three-sided shades. On the flip side she's got little computer screens like Schwarzenegger in Terminator."

Alison began giggling so hard, smiling so pretty, I didn't have the heart to remind her our own apartment is no less cramped, no less cluttered, though we do have a second bedroom available for storage. A room we lock when our mother visits (rarely), and casually refer to, if at all, as my room.

"How bad can it be," my mother asked last Thanksgiving. "Oscar never kept a messy room. Not like you."

"This is pretty bad," I said.

"How bad?"

"You don't want to know," Alison said. "He's got food in there, and laundry where laundry should never go."

3) History Lesson

For five years my sister and I have shared the same bed. It is a shameless relationship. I say that shamelessly. I use the word as a buttress to brace a slowly crumbling wall. Officially, mother knows nothing of what we are, what we've become to one another, though there are times when I'm sure she suspects.

After Phil died, we held to the notion that if we truly loved one another our kinship didn't matter. Alison prepared a short speech for our mother, titled: Taboos were made to be broken.

But I felt no urge, no need to shock the twice-widowed woman who had raised us. At that time she was already dying, or so we thought. Dying quickly. Dying more then, than now.

On my good days I still believe we have transgressed beyond our doubt. Morally, we've established a secondary orbit. When people question our devotion toward one another we fib our fibs, spin our spin.

4) Letterman

The night before our visit we were cuddled on the sofa, watching a Letterman rerun, when Alison started:

"It's not like you raped me," she said.

I didn't want to talk about it, so I said, "Alison, please."

"It's not anything she could ever understand," Alison said. "It's not even about sex."

"I'm going to bed," I said and I got up. "Good night," I said.

"Don't you see. She never had the experience. She's never been in love. She's got no life reference, the poor old witch."

"Good night," I said and shut the door.

I took off my clothes, climbed into bed, shut off the light.

Sometime later she woke me, her arms around my waist, her mouth near my ear.

"Do you know what we should tell her?"

"Who?" I said.

"We should say 'You did a good job raising us. We're no worse than anyone else.'"

She kissed the side of my mouth, placed her cool cheek against my shoulder.

We lay quiet a moment. "In some ways we're worse," I said.

I rolled and got a leg on top, pinning her. I cupped her breast, kissed her neck. "We enjoy each other too much."

5) Genesis

The first time I made love to her was an accident. Alison was twenty-nine; I was thirty-one. Sexually, we collided. There had been nothing prior, no teen-age hanky panky, no preadolescent exploration. I never molested Alison. I'll admit that once, when we were in our teens Phil, our soon-to-be stepfather, caught us together, both naked from the waist down. Later that year he married our mother, and to my knowledge, never mentioned the accidental Greek drama that he alone had witnessed. A performance which, in his lifetime, I for one considered too frightening to repeat.

Now, in our mid-thirties, Alison and I were not playing games.

If we were victims, we were victims of each other. We shared full responsibility for our passions.

Since our separate divorces we'd gone so far as to consult a lawyer-friend who, despite the dirty looks he gave me (between sly subtle glances at my sister's legs) said we weren't doing anything "blatantly illegal."

"Just don't have offspring," he said, as we were leaving. "Because then you would be in violation of several statutes."

Which told me that he had missed our point almost entirely.

6) Bewitched

"Sneak in and move a coffee table," Alison says, her nose an inch from the tomalley. "Go on," she hisses. "Drag it a couple of inches toward the doorway."

I give her a look, a dumb and crooked face that I know she can't stand.

"I dare you," she says and wrinkles her nose like Samantha in Bewitched. "Go on. Do it. Prove my theory."

In my best western drawl, I say, "Ma'am, them's the ground up livers of dead lobsters you've got your purdy nose in."

She winces and pulls back. "Smells like bad shrimp," she says, finger-combing her bangs. A strand of hair catches at the corner of her mouth. I reach for it across the table, then jerk my hand back when I hear the slap of slippers on the raw pine floors.

Into the room mother steers a wobbly tea cart on which vibrates two teakwood bowls heaped with greens and wedged tomatoes. I start to get up and she scowls. "Ass to the chair, boy. I'm not an invalid."

"He's not a boy, Mother," Alison snaps.

"Quiet, you. What's it got to do with you?"

"You needn't insult him."

"Mind your business. And sit closer to the table. Act like a lady."

"Those salads look mighty good, Mom," I say.

Alison resettles her armchair and directs her eyes at me. "He's a man," she murmurs. "A full-grown man."

"Good," my mother says. "Then he can sit like a man and eat some of this tomalley. "

I stare at my plate. "Aren't you eating with us?"

"When the hell do I ever eat? Have you seen me take a bite of nourishment since Phil died?"

"No, Ma'am," I say.

"Uh-huh," Alison says tapping her nails on the chair's arms.

Mother extracts a bottle of Russian dressing from her apron pouch. "I don't eat, but the Lord still won't take me." She aims the bottle at the ceiling. "Why, Phil? Why does he keep us apart?"

"Ma, sit," Alison says, more subdued. "Please. Sit. Watch us eat." She pats the pad of the chair beside her and my mother slumps into it as though she has just died.

For a moment she doesn't seem to be breathing, then she sighs deeply and passes the bottle. "Oscar, be a good boy and open this."

While Alison and I crunch our salads, Mom samples several mouthfuls of the tomalley, using a single cracker as a spoon.

7) Nympho

In her late teens Alison believed she suffered from nympho-mania. She began to experience frequent flashbacks. She missed half her senior year due to stomach aches and panic attacks. She suffered from recurring nightmares. Eventually she persuaded mom to spend a few thousand dollars on a therapist, only to find out that frigid nymphomaniacs are as rare as saber-toothed tigers.

At the heart of her troubles was something else. Something black. Something lost to her: "Patty cake, patty cake, baker man …"

After months of therapy she remembered events that mother and I had either forgotten or never suspected in the first place.

"… lie down and spread your legs fast as you can …"

Pumped on Prozac, she set out to seduce every hunk who wasn't gay, and I set out to make a miserable fool of myself. Which wasn't hard. I was handsome, athletic looking, comically bright, and totally stupid with women. I chased after the wrong girls. Girls I didn't like, and would quickly grow tired of. Girls nothing like Alison.

One August night I caved. I fell. She asked so politely. Perhaps out of boredom, or sympathy, or need. "Hold me," she said. "I can't sleep alone."

After that one indiscretion, (unconsummated, because Phil had burst in to tell us Hubert Humphrey had died) I decided that I was an incestuous troglodyte who shouldn't ever smoke dope with his sister. I was a mutation of the original monster, our father, who'd violated his flesh and blood daughter at seven. Barely a decade later, I was a regular chip off the old block. So I moved out. I ran.

48

For dinner we eat Pea soup, Rock Cornish hens, wild-rice, chewy green beans laced with almonds. For dessert Mother serves us two swirly cupcakes with a single pink candle stuck in each.

We sing Happy Birthday to Phil, then a chorus of "How old are you now?" When she leans in to blow out the candles, I notice a large tear escaping from beneath her dark glasses.

"Are you okay, Ma," I ask.

"My bag needs changing," she says.

"Do you want me to help you?"

"You? What the hell can you do?" Then softly to Alison: "Be a dear and fill the tub. I've got an itch I can't scratch. That's a sure sign the whole damn contraption needs changing."

One of Phil's last living acts was to install a Jacuzzi so Mother could clean and sanitize without actually touching her stoma. Alison gets up to go prepare the bath and lay out a fresh sticky-back wafer and a clean colostomy bag. My mother sits silently behind her dark glasses. I've eaten too much and my stomach is churning inside. After a long minute I remove the candle from my cupcake and lick the frosting which is horribly sweet.

"What's wrong with you today," my mother asks.

"Me? Nothing, why?"

"You seem edgy."

"Not me," I say.

"Don't think you can fool me. You're fussing and fidgeting around like you need a good stiff drink."

"I don't drink. Remember?"

I am four years clean and sober, thanks almost entirely to Alison's nurturing. I smile at the two fun-house images where my mother's eyes used to be.

"You know, Oscar, there's nothing wrong with a little taste once in a while. Just so long as you don't make a glutton of yourself. That's your problem with everything. Phil wasn't much of a drinker but he enjoyed a pousse-café from time to time."

"All set, Ma," Alison calls from the bathroom.

"Something to think about. You won't impress too many women with that stiff-assed mentality." She removes her dentures and drops them into her apron. "You're a good-looking boy but if you don't wise up you'll spend the rest of your life alone. No joke. Look at yourself.

Dependent on tips from strangers, and sponging off your poor sister is no way to live." She waggles a crooked finger. "Time to take some responsibility."

"It was my apartment first, Ma. Alison moved in with me, remember."

I watch her slowly get up, half hoping she'll fall on her face.

"Just don't count on her paying half your rent when some handsome prince comes along. She's still very attractive, ya know."

"Yea, ma."

"A lot of men would be glad to have her."

"Yes, mother."

9) Wedlock

At twenty-four, my sister married a gentleman who owned a chain of donut shops. Strictly for revenge, I married a stripper named Candy, also known as Corky, a.k.a. Candace Caldwell, born Colleen Caldwaller. Among other things she was an ex-escort. V.I.P., but permanently retired. Candy was sweet and sexy. She had fabulous hair, long legs, flawless skin. Her breasts, which were naturally full, were scheduled for augmentation.

"Wouldn't you just love a piece of hard candy," she used to tease, both professionally and in private.

I admit I enjoyed pinching her nipples while looking her straight in the eyes. I can't say that I loved her, but I adored her soft, dreamy eyes. Her eyelashes were exceptionally long, just like Alison's.

Candy was a mechanical toy, something you wound up and let spin around you. She left me flat and cold. Whereas Alison—she was a baby doll who purred like a kitten. The whole time she was married, I couldn't eat a donut without becoming sick with jealously.

10) Bath Time

While our mother bathes, Alison circles the dining room. She studies each of the pictures of our biological father, the man who brutally raped her and then hanged himself from the garage door opener with our dog's leash. These eloquently framed pictures didn't exist when Phil was alive.

A sudden creepy feeling settles in my stomach as I watch Alison click her heels and tap a fingernail against a miniature portrait of herself.

"How old do I look here," she says.

"Eight or nine, why?"

She shrugs. "No reason." Then scrutinizes the picture directly above: a smiling, waving Phil posing beside a fish big as a surfboard. "Oscar, do you think you'll ever become bored and leave me?"

She spins to face me, her black eyes, lustrous, sad and gentle.

She smiles, showing off her brilliant white teeth, forcing her cheekbones high. The shape of her jaw melds perfectly with her small sharp nose, her bee-stung lips.

I watch her mouth, see her pink tongue protrude like the head of a snake. "Don't even think about it."

"What?" she says, rapid blinking, smoothing her dress against her thighs. She sits with a twitch of her ass and rests her hand on my lap.

"Careful," I say trapping her hand against my thigh.

"Prude." She withdraws her hand, crosses her legs and folds her arms, pretending to pout. She lifts her breasts with a sigh. "You didn't eat your cupcake."

Before I can answer she pulls me close and slides her tongue into my mouth.

I put my hands on her shoulder and move her away. "Don't start. Remember where we are."

She gives me a sly wink. "Oh, I know where we are," she says sliding lower in her chair.

Next thing I know she is under the table, all business. My trousers unzipped, my penis exposed, she persuades me with kisses and licks. Then she is pure suction, and my resistance fades. I close my eyes, gripping the table's edge. When I feel myself getting close, I bite the inside of my cheek, my lip, my tongue. It finally takes Alison's hand to muffle my guttural growl.

"Alison!" our mother calls.

My sister smiles up at me from between my legs. The tablecloth frames her face like a veil.

"Alison!" our mother calls.

"Get up," I rasp. "I don't believe you did that."

"Why. She can't climb out by herself."

"I don't believe I let you."

"You didn't let me. And you didn't make me. That's my point."

"Alison! Help me with this god damned thing."

"Coming, Ma."

—

51

She smooths her dress in the doorway, then steps back into the room and uses a portrait of our father as a mirror.

"That little show was strictly for your pleasure, and Phil's entertainment. "She picks and fluffs out her hair, then dabs on fresh lipstick. She puckers and blows a kiss toward the photo. "And any other spiritual presence that might be watching."

11) Jersey Jack

Last Easter, mother invited Phil's "baby" brother from Jersey; Jack Burns—an oval-headed man with crooked teeth. When he arrived Mother made Alison answer the door, then acted surprised that Jack had brought along his nephew, Warren.

"Warren, meet my Alison," Mother said.

"We met at the funeral," Warren said.

He had wide shoulders and oily hair, a tiny scar beneath one eye.

I got slowly to my feet, then stood there, waiting to be introduced.

"Warren was a pall bearer," Mother said.

Alison's eyes, fixed on Warren, seemed to come slowly into focus.

She smiled politely and shook his hand. I felt my heart lurch as though it had torn away from a major artery.

After dinner and coffee, after dessert and more coffee, after hearing all about Warren's tragic divorce, Mother suggested Alison give "our young guest" a tour of the grounds.

Grounds, I thought. What grounds?

"Warren is an avid bird watcher," Mother said.

"Oh, really. Then he'll love the swamp, "Alison said, in her little girl voice.

What could I say? I angled my chair by a window and watched them set out toward a slimy backyard pond surrounded by red and yellow flowers. I watched them disappear into a patch of thick overgrowth. I wasn't worried. Let the poor bastard think he's onto something.

I drank coffee and half-listened to Jack tell me about his career as a minor league umpire. "Just couldn't crack the big time," he said at the conclusion of each anecdote.

I continually shook my head at him, trying to match his sadness.

Hours later, on the long ride home, I asked Alison if she had enjoyed her walk.

Her tanned and freckled shoulders gleamed, bare above a peach strapless dress.

She said, "We saw a humming bird and the guy went nuts."

I snickered. "Anything else?"

"Yea. The clown tried to slip his hand up my dress. But then he apologized. Then he cried and sobbed a little, telling me about his marriage. Then he tried to kiss me. He claimed he was disturbed by my beauty."

"Did you?"

"Did I what?"

"Did you kiss him?"

"No. But I thought about it. I felt sorry for the guy. He's a mess."

I nodded and drove on in silence. I remembered all the years I had hated my sister because she wouldn't fuck me.

12) Clean Up

While Alison plays nurse, I clean the kitchen and polish the stove. I run the dishwasher to mask the sounds of the garbage disposal grinding bones. I mop the floor, dancing with the mop, sashaying into the bathroom to mop there. I get the whole place looking shipshape, then go in to kiss my mother goodbye, to thank her for a lovely dinner, but my sister touches a finger to her lips. "Too late," she says, and tugs the chain on the reading lamp.

We lock up the house as though no one lives there, double checking every door and window.

Driving home, past cornfields and lavish country homes, a paper sack of leftovers between us, I ask Alison what a pousse-café is. She shrugs, examining her fingernails. "I'm pretty sure it's a drink. But I'd have to ask Freddie."

Freddie? It's a name I've never heard her mention.

We rumble across the planks of a narrow covered bridge then emerge to see the glow of city lights. "Freddie who," I say, "Is this someone I should be concerned about?"

"Uh huh. And handsome as a prince, too," Alison says.

13) Blood Appointment

At home there are fourteen messages on the answering machine— all of them for Alison. Six are from a small creepy man who followed

---

her home from work one afternoon and then somehow got our number. (After much to-do, he was permanently banned from the Merit Cafe where Alison waits tables, and I work the bar.) Seven are from former friends of mine—old buddies and pals who think they are doing me a huge favor by courting my sister. The very last message is from our mother, and less than an hour old. She tells us she awoke in the dark with no idea of where she or anyone else was. She thanks Alison for cleaning her kitchen, then reminds her of a "blood appointment." "Not that I've got any blood left," she says. "I guess I can skip if you don't want to take the time. Call me. Let me know."

After playing the tape a second time, stopping the machine before the last, we tear at each other's clothes. Alison's hungry kisses smother my lips. We fall onto the bed to make love with adolescent frenzy. It is warm, glorious, exciting. I ride her hips for what seems like hours. I don't stop until I'm sure I've exhausted her. Until she claws at my back, laughingly pleading for me to stop. Only then do I come.

Afterwards, lying soft inside of her, my face buried in her hair, I say, "Alison, honey. Are you happy?"

"Never happier," she says coolly. But the tone is too close to her waitress voice, equivalent to "Thank you, have a nice day."

I roll off of her, on to my back, staring up at nothing.

"Let's call in sick tomorrow. We'll take a drive. Walk the beaches."

"I wish," she says. And after a short pause, "We need the money."

In the dark we hold each other. The euphoria that comes after sex is gone. I have this foreboding inside, this shivering cold sensation. We are brother and sister again, nestled in the same bed. When I start to cry, she pulls me closer, her fingers gently caressing my spine. "Hey," she says. "Hey. What's this?"

I tell her I don't know what it is, that I don't know what's wrong with me. Then I let her kiss my neck, my hair.

I say, "Lately I'm having a lot of trouble liking myself."

"You're not so bad. I'd marry you in a second," she says.

14) Bidet

She holds me until my sobbing stops, until I am nearly asleep, almost dreaming; then she spoils it by getting up. I pretend not to notice, to snore quietly. I watch her through the hazy slits of my eyes, but I know where she is going, what she's up to. Last Sunday I found the thing wrapped in a towel. I traced the listing on her VISA statement—a bidet

---

54

purchased via mail-order. The morning I discovered it I thought of taking a Greyhound bus as far as I could go. I thought of dialing my mom and telling her who'd been fucking her little girl.

Now, after sex she disappears into the bathroom to wash away my sperm and our sin. I don't see the point. There is no point. She's had a complete hysterectomy; I've had a vasectomy. We are barren and godless.

I fix the sheets and wait. I listen to the water running. This bidet thing is something that needs talking through. We mustn't keep secrets from one another. No more darkness—we agreed. My blood heats up, listening to the water. Suddenly I feel chilled to the bone. When the water stops I get up and spread another blanket on the bed, then another. Then a half-sized comforter my mother gave Alison for Christmas. Wrapped up like a mummy, I listen to the quiet splash of water and I try to imagine what it must be like being her—a breathtaking beauty who judges herself merely pretty; a size five who complains she's a blimp. I wonder what she might be thinking, sitting there, cleansing herself of her brother's sterile semen. I shudder a breath as the toilet flushes. I close my eyes. The whine of the pipes makes me dizzy.

15) Limo Dream

I dream of my ex-wife, Candy. I dream that she is my mother—young, attractive, healthy. Alison is driving us in a white stretch limo. I sit in the back, dressed as a waiter. On my tux is a name-tag. Alison wears a wedding dress. She races the engine which is streaming black smoke. "We're all right," she says. "We turn left up ahead. Right? Left, then a hard right."

"That girl can't see where she's going," says Candy, who is wearing my mother's black goggles, her flowery robe. I'm about to tell her she's not my mother, that the woman driving us is my sister, my heart's desire, when I see flames bursting from the engine reflected in her black bug-eyes. I wake up sweating. I'm on the wrong side of the bed again. The clock on the nightstand glows: 1:49 A.M.

16) Two A.M.

The phone rattles me awake. I pick it up between rings and my mother's scratchy—but very much alive—voice hollers into my ear: "Oscar. What's wrong? Where have you been? Why didn't Alison call?

55

I've been worried to death. I'm sitting by my police scanner with all the lights on. Where's your sister?. Let me talk to Alison? Is Alison all right?"

"She's fine, mom. She's right here."

"Right where?"

"In her room, in her bed."

Alison pops her head up and props on an elbow, her sleepy face hidden behind a heavy veil of hair.

"Who are you calling," she says and I bump the phone against her arm.

"It's for you. Be careful."

"I had a dream about Phil," my mother informs us as the mouthpiece falls into the folds of the blankets.

"What is it?," Alison says, her eyes still closed. "Stop poking me."

"Snap to," I say. "You're on. Showtime. It's her."

"Who," Alison says, swatting the covers. "Why are you waking me?"

Our heads bump as we grasp for the phone, lifting it together, cradling our mother's shrill cry between us: "Oscar? Alison! Oh, Phil! Oh Lord, where have you taken my babies?"

At the Factory

I work a four-day week, four ten-hour shifts. I can't complain. All my Fridays, all my weekends, every major holiday off. I work the line. All I know is the line. It's what I was hired for, trained for—which was plain dumb luck, because all that's left now is the line—just the line and the crew on the loading dock. Big shots up in Houston pushed everything else over the border. Three hundred miles dead south. Weavers, braiders, dyers, tippers, inspectors—all gone. Two hundred and eighty-six jobs.

Outsourcing, they call it.

I call it a sin.

Loading dock they couldn't touch. Because of the union. I ain't union. Nobody on the line is union. There are fifty of us left. Quotas keep climbing. One or all of us could go any day.

The morning I got the call, I said to the line boss, Hey Fred, mind if I stumble in late tomorrow?

Tomorrow, he said. What's tomorrow?

We were in the break room, a long narrow space, formerly an empty corridor, and well on its way to being one again. After the big layoff they sealed the cafeteria, donated all the tables and benches to some orphanage. Fred and I stood between a double row of vending machines.

He frowned at the mention of my being late as he studied his clip board.

Wait a minute. Hold on. You don't work Fridays, he said.

I said, I know that, Fred. I realize that.

Then I said, My mother just died. Her funeral is in the morning.

That moved him back a step. He leaned against the soda machine and studied his clip board some more. I honestly don't believe he knew what to say.

I said, Hell, it's no big deal, Fred. Everybody dies. Right?

Sure, he said.

I said, I thought maybe if it's okay with you I might go to the funeral and then wander in here. You know. Sometimes it's better I work and not think too much.

He studied my face. He looked at me hard. Then he agreed that sometimes working was better than thinking. He showed me his clipboard. He slid his finger across my name, and then down.

There. That's Friday. See. He shook his head. No Xs.

An X represented a machine with no operator. If there were machines available Fred was authorized to give hours to anyone who wanted them. I told him if I didn't work I'd drink.

He kept frowning, kept shaking his head.

I said, I'll end up crazy drunk with a bunch of creepy old aunts and uncles who believe Elvis is a Saint and still alive and that aliens do nightly flybys and that JFK is hiding in a bat cave somewhere in Montana.

I then made mention of several additional mostly old horribly creepy Hispanic people none of whom I can stand to be around and one of whom has a plaster of Paris impression of Big Foot's big footprint hanging on her living room wall.

You a big drinker, Carl, Fred said.

I told him I hadn't had a drop in four years, honest to God, and that I would consider it a personal favor if this one time he could please cut me some slack, which is a stale joke around a shoelace factory.

How long you been sober? For real.

One hundred and twenty one days, I said.

That's still a lot of days, said Fred.

It's my new world record, I said.

He put his hand on my shoulder and steered me over to one of the coffee machines. He said he was terribly sorry about my loss. Then he fed the machine a few coins. He bought me a coffee.

Listen, he said. Tell you what. Coming in tomorrow is pretty much up to you, okay? Whatever you want to do.

He smiled and I shook his hand. I thanked him. I told Fred he was a swell guy.

Then I emptied six sugar packets into my coffee and stirred it with a pencil. On the walk back to the line he asked if my mother's death had been sudden.

She died this morning, I said.

He nodded. Then he said what he had meant to ask was had she been ill for a long time.

I shrugged. You're asking the wrong person, Fred. I haven't seen the woman in a dog's age.

How old?

Not very, I said. She had me at fifteen. I was born on this side, about 800 feet over the border, which makes me one hundred percent legal, and would have made her a citizen too if she'd stayed. Mostly my aunts raised me. They did a good job.

But then I ran out of aunts.

58

He sipped his coffee and looked everywhere but at me. I think he knew I wouldn't come in.

***

The next afternoon, five or six hours after the funeral, I called in. I asked to speak to the line boss. It was late, right around shift change. I had to have Fred paged. Every half minute the receptionist came back on the line. Ace Shoelace corporation, can I help you?

Each time I told her the same thing: I'm holding for Fred.

One moment, I'll connect you.

This went on and on like a bad dream.

When Fred finally picked up, I told him how terribly sorry I was that I hadn't made it in. I apologized for letting him down. I said I felt stupid, and that I hoped he hadn't actually been counting me in the numbers.

Who is this, he said.

Carl, I said.

Carl? Which Carl?

Carl with the dead mother, I said.

It came out like a sob and for a moment I thought he'd hung up. Then he said he hadn't forgotten about me, that in fact the whole plant had been informed of my personal tragedy and everyone, management included, was deeply saddened by my sudden loss.

That did it for me. I lost it. I lost it badly. I told Fred the truth was my mother had been a cheap Mexican whore her whole life, had never given two shits about me, and that right now she was dancing with the devil in some cantina in hell.

I said, I know this to be a fact, Fred. Because I'm in her sorry excuse for a house and it is full of crucifixes and creeps. Fred, they are everywhere, like roaches. They're spilling out onto the road.

Then I explained my simple yet elaborate plan to throw up on anyone who tried to wrestle the phone away from me.

Fred said that he couldn't talk anymore because it was shift change. He said he was sorry.

You don't like me very much do you, Fred?

Why do you say that?

Because this is the longest conversation we've ever had.

The next one will be longer, Fred said. I promise. Then he asked when I was scheduled again.

Monday, I said.

See you on Monday, Carl.

Hey, Fred, what about tomorrow, I said, but he'd already hung up.

***

My mother is dead, my boss feels bad, news travels fast as my uncle Salvador could make them I drank them down licking salt, sucking lime, You want another, Sal said, and I said Sal, damn it Sal, make me another mother, mine is dead Sal, my mother is dead, and he pulled me by my shirt-collar, slapped me, hard on the chin, almost a punch, so I said alright Sal, I said okay all you creeps, get out of my mother's house, get out you fuckers, I want you out of my sight you hypocrites, you miserable rat turds, at that point I couldn't see them or anything, blurred by drink but I was screaming go, out, leave, get your asses out of my mother's house, and the next thing I know I'm on my back coming to in the Emergency room which is really a two bit undercover abortion clinic, a two-room shack with just one doctor and one nurse and I'm there with Sal, my uncle Sal, who suddenly doesn't look so good, so I'm asking the nurse is his heart strong enough to take this, so the doctor gives him the once over, and the doctor says not good, you better take these, give him two, never more than two mind you, four times a day all day, so all day Saturday I tried but Sal said no pills, Carl, no thank you no more god damn pills, but the doctor said I said, and my uncle said to hell with the doctor, Carl, get it through your thick skull your beautiful mother is dead.

And that told me something about Sal that I had never wanted to know, like it or not.

***

First thing Monday morning I told Fred all about the ER. I related every part of the story that I could remember. He had called or I had called, I forget which. I don't remember the phone waking me up but I don't remember dialing, either. I was on a binge, but I didn't tell Fred that. I told him my uncle Sal drove us back across the border and carried me dead drunk up three flights of stairs. I reminded Fred that I weighed almost two hundred pounds. My uncle's about one ten, one twenty tops. It could have killed him, I said.

Fred said, it should have.

I cleared my throat.

I said, Sal's gone now. He left his pills and some money that he said my mother wanted me to have, and a grainy black and white photograph of her cradling something in her arms. He says it's me she's holding but you can't tell, not really. I'll bring it in, let you decide for yourself.

Fred said he thought it might be a good idea for me to take a couple of days off. Think things over, he said. Get your act together. At a time like this by your family's side is really where you want to be, Carl. Are you hearing me, son?

I said, Shit Fred, I ain't got no family. And I'm never very good at times like these, which is why I like to work.

I hear ya, Fred said.

By then I was sniffling snots and bawling like a brat. Fred kept talking but I couldn't make out half the words. When I went to move the phone to my other ear I dropped it. I kept reaching and fumbling the thing because my hands were wet and I was trembling so bad. When I finally got the phone back to my ear I figured Fred was gone for sure.

I screamed his name three times before he answered.

Easy Carl. Easy! Take a couple of breaths.

I didn't think I was going to make it. I couldn't get any air into my lungs.

Then Fred said: On second thought maybe you better get your ass in here.

He said, I hate to make demands on a grieving son, a man who just lost his mother, but I've got three machines sitting idle, Houston is screaming in my ear, and I've got fresh quotas to fill. You know how it is. Can you handle two machines at once? Can you do that for me, son? Can I count on you to help me out?

Sure, I told him, I can do that for you, Fred. Hell, I said, what else am I good for?

Tomorrow Isn't Friday

The first time my father's quick-change scam flubs I'm in a liquor store down on Gannon Street. I'm working alone, which is a mistake, and I'm stoned, which the clerk behind the register recognizes in an instant. He shoos me away like he's waving off one of the ten-billion flies buzzing the place.

With a gap-toothed grin he says "Nice try, pal. Next!"

Right away I get confused. My father's patterned never-fail scam misfires in front of this dork, this nobody, this pimply-faced dweeb with blue-framed glasses. His smirk—a creepy, knowing look, a charge of stupidity more than an accusation of criminal behavior—generates a dull pain behind my eyeballs that shoots straight to the back of my head.

I step away from the counter and try to regroup. I must have done something wrong so I run through the steps again, my heart clanging like there's a buoy bell bobbing between my lungs. What am I buying? Jesus Christ, I didn't buy anything.

"You're blocking the lady," the kid says.

The scam doesn't work if you don't make a purchase. How in hell could it? There's no change, no transaction to work from. I pocket the twenty and step to one side, allowing a woman customer to slide up to cash and carry. I swallow a giant mouthful of refrigerated air and watch the clerk ring her up.

She's buying four bottles of white wine. (I could buy wine.) She asks the kid for a carton of Camels. (I could buy cigarettes.) She's wearing a light coat and dark nylons; nice legs, nice shoes. Her hair is short but she looks a lot like my mother, that generation, that look.

When she leaves, I follow. We exit single-file through the automatic doors into the soft heat and I watch her get into her car. She folds her legs in, pulls the door shut, starts her engine. I tell her to have a nice day but she doesn't give me so much as a glance. After she drives off I stand there like a dummy and try to find the sun, but it's just a haze between buildings. When my pulse drops to normal I try coming in again. But I'm too buzzed. Twice I make the electric eye on the door announce my reentry, and twice I approach the register to begin from the beginning. It doesn't matter what I buy, but I don't give anything to the clerk, or ask for anything on the shelves behind the counter. He's about my age, my height and weight, with a bowl cut hairstyle and a round face. His chin is pink with pimples. He stares at my twenty, grinning like we went to scam school together. A sign suspended on a chain tells it all: No Credit. No checks. No Rest Rooms. No Change.

It's a high counter so who knows, maybe he toe-taps a buzzer, or fingers a switch that causes sirens and flashing lights to go off in the back room, because in no time a tall silver-haired man opens a door and comes out. He stands beside a pyramid of cheap vodka. Behind his wire spectacles he's sizing me up, watching me mope. I tour the beer- and wine-section for the fifth or sixth time, flapping my folded twenty against my knuckles; I start to sweat. I strike a pose for the security cameras. Then I have a flash of watching myself being handcuffed on some idiot cop TV show. The old guy takes off his glasses and slants his caterpillar eyebrows. "Problem, son?"

I think he's talking to me because at me is where he is staring. All my standard excuses start streaming through my brain.

But the kid behind the counter answers, "No problem here, Mister Sirois," hiding half his face behind a fat paperback with a green dragon on the cover. He's flipping pages too fast and I'm sure he's mouthing something to the old man from behind the book. My high is 98% gone. My senses generate a code red so I blow a kiss to one of the cameras and head for the door. Just to be safe, I detour, stack a dollar in quarters on the counter, snap a 99-cent bag of cashews from the rack, and exit through the glass doors. I walk home. The elevator is still out of order. I climb four flights in the heat, tonguing cashew crud from my teeth.

Ma's TV is off and she's knitting in front of the window fan which is streaming warm air on high, lifting her lacquered hair up and away like a wing. She doesn't look at me, doesn't say hi. She works her needles, unraveling yarn from one of Dad's old sweaters.

"You smell sweet, like dope," she says.

"I told you. My friends smoke it."

"Get some new friends," Ma says.

I go into the bathroom, and splash water on my face. I make a cup with my hands and slurp a mouthful. Then I splash more water on my neck and on my eyes and I run my wet hands through my hair. I push and squeeze at a new pimple until it hurts, then I go back and stand in the doorway. I comb my hair with my fingers and listen to the hum of the fan and the clicking sound the knitting needles make.

After a minute she says, "Did you forget what day it is?"

I don't answer.

"It's Friday," Ma says.

"I know."

"You got something for me."

I shake my head.

"You don't?"

"Not today."

"Why is that?"

"I'll have something for you tomorrow."

I walk over and turn on the TV, then fall down on my cot. "We're shoplifting at the Mini-Mart in the morning. Kelly and me. Kelly's my diversion. We'll bring you back those little powdered donuts you like."

She knits while I flick through the channels.

"You don't scam high," she says. "You know better. You'll end up like your father.."

"I'm not high," I tell her, which is the truth now, because my buzzing brain has turned to mud. I shut off the TV.

She clicks her needles. "Where's my money, big shot?"

"I'll have money for you tomorrow."

"Tomorrow isn't Friday," she says.

She knits slow and steady. I stretch out on my cot and think about kicking my shoes off. On the floor by her chair the sleeve of my father's sweater spins as parts disappear.

Ma says, "Shut that damn TV off if you're not watching it, please."

"It's off," I say.

"You're not paying the bills around here."

"It's off."

"I can feel it heating up the room."

"The TV is off," I say.

She looks up, blinks. "Thank you," she says.

Ten seconds later Kelly stumbles in with her arm around a man in bib overalls.

"Don't anybody help me," she says.

She's wearing sunglasses with blue lenses in yellow cat-eye frames but not on her face. The glasses are in her hair, a helmet of bleached white curls and waves. Her makeup is precise. She resembles a movie star on vacation.

The guy she's holding up looks to be in bad shape, like he died once already. He has blotches all over his face, and a sore on his lip and a dime-size scab in the hinge of his arm. He's a putrid fellow, with a clean shaven skull. Rocco is stitched in looping script across the wide pocket.

"Jack, give Rocco your bed," my sister says.

"Don't you drop that sack of shit in my bed."

64

"Watch your mouth," Ma says. "He's still a guest."

"Screw him," I say. "Let him sleep on the floor."

Rocco perks his chin up. His eyes are slits. "En Ef Double you, Johnny!"

"What's he saying to me?"

"No Fucking Way," Kelly says.

Ma chuckles and says, "Who is he?"

"Rocco's a poet," Kelly says.

"Where'd you find a poet around here?"

"In the park. He bought me supper and watched me eat."

I'm tapping my pockets, feeling for my knife, but I'm not finding it.

"En Ef Double you, Johnny. En Ef Double you!" Rocco says.

I feel my neck heating up. Where in hell is my knife?

"He has an ATM card," Kelly says. "I watched him use it."

Ma chuckles while she knits. "I bet you did."

Kelly steps and nearly drops him. "You could help me, you jerk!"

"Help your sister with her friend," Ma says.

I step away from the cot as Kelly moves Rocco forward, struggling to hold him up. She's taller by a foot. He's thin and hard to look at. Already his sore is oozing something that could be blood.

"Drop him on the floor," I say.

"Put 'cha right down here," Kelly says. "There you go, there you are, honey."

"Easy Johnny, Easy now," Rocco says with a shuddering breath.

"Who the hell is Johnny?" Ma says.

Kelly untangles her arm from his bulk. "Pay no attention." She wipes blood from her fingers onto Rocco's shirtsleeve. "He says that to everybody."

Rocco folds down slow and curls into himself. He lies clumsily on his side, and Kelly lifts his legs onto the cot. She gently turns his head so his face is showing. He looks broken laying there, then Kelly brings his knees higher, arranges him in a fetal position. "Rocco? You still with us, baby?"

The man's going to die on my bed and no amount of washing and scrubbing takes out that stain. Tonight I'll sleep in a chair, or on the floor, or maybe I'll walk the streets, zigzagging through decent neighborhoods, until my feet get so tired I just drop down on somebody's perfectly groomed lawn. Tomorrow, or the next day, I'll look for honest work.

65

"Rocco? Honey?" Kelly says, and gives him a violent shake. He's sprawled sideways, open eyed, but deathly still. My nose starts to twitch. The newly dead let go of everything, all fluids, solids, gases, anything they've got stored. They leak it out within seconds.

"Give him another minute," Mom says.

Meanwhile his overalls are trapped, twisted tight, caught awkwardly beneath him, and his wallet is popping, his wallet is just bursting to get out.

ABCDEFGH

(A)

I met her at a CYO dance that I wasn't supposed to be at because I was neither a dancer nor a Catholic. Her name was Donna. She wasn't pretty and she wasn't rich but her daddy owned a business and her family lived in a big house with a wraparound porch, which made them rich in my book.

After one slow dance, before I even knew her name, she let me French kiss her between the air conditioner and the Coke machine. She had a wide mouth overcrowded with perfectly straight teeth and a tongue like an angry snake.

(B)

Eighteen months later, I suggested we climb a mountain, a small mountain. I studied some maps, found a low peak. A short, zigzagging, two-mile hike. She had scaled a few mountains prior, and I had camped on a couple of steep hillsides with the Scouts, but this was our first mountain together. We planned to kiss at the summit. She didn't know about the ring.

To be safe we had each invited a pair of friends to climb along and witness our affections, and to help carry sandwiches, water and wine, and add to the general spirit and to the joy. Plus, I wanted pictures taken of me proposing on one knee.

In a clearing marked "Last Trash Can" we broke for lunch. Cold air swallowed us up. People and warnings started floating down. Hikers hurried past us, shouting downhill. The weather had shifted. There was wind and ice and snow above the tree line. Ruddy-faced climbers with backpacks and knitted caps turned back. We had nothing. We were six kids in denim jackets. We were children.

(C)

At the altar, while reciting my vows, which I had written a week earlier and thoroughly memorized—a sort of long rambling prose poem expressing loyalty, devotion, joy, happiness, really sappy stuff, most of it penned while I was stoned—about halfway through, my throat tightened up and my voice broke into this shrill falsetto one might expect from a

---

67

prepubescent choir boy. My knees and elbows began to shake; one leg felt ready to buckle; I thought I was going down faster than you can say "Take this ring."

My bride detected my malfunction in a heartbeat. Under the pretense of adjusting her veil, she poked her elbow into my ribcage. The jab made me flinch, straighten, and gulp for breath.

Turns out a little air was all I needed.

Two or three slow breaths later, still shaky but less woozy, I prepared to continue from where I'd left off. Problem was my mind had gone blank. Though I knew my lines by heart, and could have recited them from the beginning, mentally I'd lost my place. For a long moment the church was as quiet as a funeral. The priest wavered his eyebrows. The pretty bride shuffled her feet.

At a traditional Catholic ceremony the veil remains down until the very end, so I couldn't see Donna's face, but fearing another jab I coughed to clear my throat then skipped over everything I had written, summing up in a croaky but level voice that I'd love Donna all the days of my life.

No one but the priest had reviewed my notes, so no one else in attendance was the wiser. The thing is, I left out a substantial portion of what I had intended to say that morning, much of it gushy and sentimental, though all of it heartfelt. Considering how things ended up—the marriage imploded after eighteen months—that's just as well. More than a dozen people were videotaping, making a permanent record, and I'd really hate for Donna—or anyone for that matter—to know what a love sick fool I was back then.

(D)

Our first weekend back from the honeymoon we went to a Chinese restaurant on Mineral Spring Avenue in Pawtucket. We sat in a padded booth, waiting for menus, staring at each other across the Formica table-top with our placemats showing the signs of the Chinese zodiac.

I didn't know anything about the Chinese zodiac but within minutes I discovered my new wife had been born in the year of the tiger while I had been born in the year of the snake.

When I pointed that out to her, she didn't seem impressed.

An Asian girl brought us menus. They were like a giant children's book: six pages of block type surrounded by drawings of red dragons attacking Chinese sailing ships.

"Are we going to get a bunch of side dishes to split or eat separate meals?"

"I don't know what I want," I said.

I remember her lighting a cigarette in that hollow-cheek fashion that she always used to light her cigarettes, every one. She was six weeks pregnant, already hurting the baby's lungs, heart and brain, but we didn't know that yet.

Streaming smoke at me, she said, "Why the look?" and I kept staring, straining my muscles to balance the corners of my face, thinking, God damn, this crude smile is going to collapse and give me away, tip my hand, reveal my honest feelings. And that was the first time I admitted to myself that we weren't going to make it, no matter what I said. So I recorded that moment like a history lesson, taking special note of the brief life we had shared.

(E)

I was having trouble finding a place I could afford. Every night I slept on the couch. She still did my laundry and made my meals. I still helped with the baby. Day after day we talked about how things would be after. These discussions were uncommonly civil and frank. I began to look forward to them.

I think we were chatting about how often I would visit and how much I would pay, when out of nowhere she slapped me.

I could take a slap in those days. It didn't faze me. I didn't do more than blink.

After a long silence she raised her arm like she was winding up for a second shot, then slowly brought her hand to her mouth. Tears streamed down her cheeks.

"Hurt your hand?" I said.

She nodded, trembling all over.

"Let me see."

"It's all right," she said.

"Let me have a look."

She shook her head no, then extended the hand, limp, listless. I held it, rubbed my thumb across her knuckles, then turned it over and looked at her palm. It was flushed red but it looked all right.

"It hurts," she said.

"Can you move your fingers?"

She moved one after another until she'd moved them all. Her eyes looked raw.

"You know I'll never forgive you," she said. "You know that, right?"

(F)

My first night in that cramped, attic room I didn't sleep. Not a wink. I simply lay on my back, still as a corpse, sunk deep into the bowed, rank smelling mattress. I thought about a great number of things, including my wife, while listening to the sounds of mice scurrying through the walls. Of course, I didn't know they were mice. I mistook the scratchy noise for the tapping of summer rain upon the roof.

The room I'd rented was a windowless space adjacent to a filthy kitchen shared by eight other roomers, all men, all of us running away from something. Each night mice traveled past my room and squeezed through holes and cracks to raid our kitchen. Previous roomers had plugged many of these entrances with cardboard and scraps of wood, but they hadn't gotten all of them, and each night the mice came and went pretty much as they pleased.

Every morning we would assess the damage—the half-gnawed boxes of corn flakes, oatmeal, pasta. We'd follow the path of mouse droppings back to some new entry point. Then seal that hole as best we could.

There was more to it, of course. The agonizing day-to-day, the petty arguments and drunken fights. Sometimes a death due to a heart attack, or an overdose. But essentially that is how we lived, tracing trails of mouse shit, discovering holes then blocking them, setting traps, spreading poison, working collectively, until someone moved out or got themselves evicted, or returned to his wife, leaving the rest of us to carry on, battling things we could not see.

(G)

One Saturday, shortly after all the papers had been filed and we were just waiting for the court to make it official, she called and said, "What are you doing?"

I said, "Laundry. Why?"

She said, "Feel like chatting?"

And the way she overextended her syllables made me suspect she had been drinking.

"Where's the baby," I said.

"At my mom's. Why?"

"How is she," I said.

"My mother?"

"No. My daughter."

After a long silence, she said, "We're all absolutely fine, thank you for asking."

And that came out bitter and cold, like she wasn't quite drunk enough. So I explained how things worked with a shared laundry room in a house with eight other tenants.

"Oh, poor you," she said.

I said, "Is there something special you wanted?"

And she said, "Yeah. I wanted you to know that somehow someway I'm going to make you fall in love with me again."

"What would be the point of that," I said.

"Just to make you hurt," she said.

(H)

On the fourth of July I stopped by the house to hand over money and drop off a box of sparklers for my daughter. She was far too young to hold one herself but I thought she'd enjoy watching the fizzle and spark.

Naturally, Donna wanted to talk again, even though there was nothing left to talk about.

And wouldn't be, not for a good long while. I had signed a lease, put down a security deposit, advanced two months' rent.

She nursed the baby to sleep, showing more breast than she needed to. Then she set the kid on the Lazy Boy and boxed her in with a couch pillow. We split a beer and smoked a thin joint. I wondered where she had found money to buy marijuana.

The smoke tasted cool, sweet, thick. Really potent shit. We got goofy high and I suggested we go outside and burn the sparklers. She said, "Sure, but I want to show you something first."

Then she led me by the hand into the bedroom. She crossed her arms around my neck and said, "Miss me?"

I didn't know what to answer so I kissed her very hard on the mouth. But after five minutes I got sick of kissing her. I pushed her onto the bed and rolled her over. She pretended she was dead. I lifted her skirt and she propped up on her elbows. "Careful, that's silk," she said.

Her underwear was printed with rows of pink hearts. I pulled the fabric to one side. "Let me do it," she said.

It had been months since we'd touched with any degree of kindness. I could not remember the last time we'd made love in daylight. I heard the baby squeak from the other room. The kid was waking up, so I put my hand on the back of D's neck and pushed her face into the pillows.

She raised her ass a little higher.

"Be nice," she said.

Those words became the last in a long series of serious miscommunications between us.

The Dog Barked

The clap sounded like distant thunder. The bedroom filled with light. The window's shade sputtered as it flapped around its roller.

"Rise and shine," Patty said.

Lee shifted onto his back. He tugged the top-sheet above his head. "What are you doing? What day is it?"

"It's Sunday," Patty said. She popped the shade on the second window.

"For God's sake," said Lee.

"Oh, don't be an old grump," Patty said.

Lee groaned beneath the covers. "You know I hate sun. The glare aggravates my condition. Those aren't my words. That's my surgeon's observations."

"You have to hear my dream," Patty said.

She was poised, hands on hips, in the slanting shadow between the windows.

Lee stretched the sheet into a one-man tent. "Pull those shades and I'm all ears."

Patty shifted her weight onto one hip. "Don't hide, Lee. It's after seven. I made coffee."

"Seven? Christ!" He made the sheet puff like a sail.

"It's your own fault," said Patty.

After a short silence Lee lowered the sheet and aligned the edge with his nose. His forehead was thick with creases, his eyes squeezed to slits. "My head is throbbing and my eyelids aren't working."

"If you're looking for sympathy, look elsewhere," Patty said.

Lee performed a number of eye stretching squints. He was forty, with stark white hair and a sharply angular face. He squinted at Patty who had turned her back to him to face the sun.

"I tell you, Lee, this dream is a real breakthrough. I'm excited by it." Her hair was loose, damp from her shower. Sunlight glowed around its edges. "I think it's a sign of new current."

"New current?"

"A new direction, a genuine shift. I can't wait to share it with group. Sit up. I'll tell you about it."

"Coffee first," Lee said.

"It's brewing," Patty said. She made a quick show of loosening, then tightening her robe. She was younger by a decade, a tall, slender woman with straight hair past her jaw line. "Bring us some while I brush my teeth and take my pills. You are not going to believe this dream."

Three or five or ten minutes later Lee heard his wife come back into the room.

"Bum!" Patty said.

Lee dragged a pillow over his face. "Caw Fee!" he said. "Please!"

"I should take your picture," Patty said. "Post it outside your office. Let all your students see what a professor Polliwog you really are."

Lee felt the mattress dip as she settled in beside him. She put a hand on his hip.

"Six martinis," she said. "What were you thinking?"

Lee groaned beneath the pillow. "No lectures before coffee."

Patty pulled her pillow away. "Get up Polliwog!"

Lee swung his legs over the side. He got up without looking at Patty. He followed his feet on the carpet until he found the doorframe, then the railing on the stairs. The lower rooms were still dark. A black German Shepherd—less than six months old—charged at him from the shadow of a potted plant.

Lee opened the door and waved at the animal.

"Go on," he said. "Go bite the heads off the rest of my roses."

He watched the dog run straight to the front gate and lift on its hind legs. The shadow of the house ended there, and the dog's front paws and head took on a softer, lighter tone.

Lee shadowed his face with one hand and watched a passing car; then he shut the door and went into the kitchen. He shielded his eyes as he crossed an area where dust floated in the light. He poured two cups of coffee. He pulled a deep breath then bent his knees and took a tiny sip from each cup. He felt shaky going up the stairs.

In the bedroom, Patty had straightened and tucked the sheets. She was stretched out on his side of the bed with all the pillows behind her. The window shades were at half mast. Everything looked clean and crisp. She said: "So, I woke up. My heart pounding. I felt cold."

"What time?"

"Quarter to four."

Lee nodded. He stood by the bed and handed her cup to her.

"The dog barked," Patty said. "He woke me." She took a sip of coffee. "He might need to go out again."

"It's done," Lee said. "Did you dream about the dog?"

"No," said Patty, pushing out breath. "But he was right there. He barked at me. He's never done that. Then he ran downstairs and chased his tail for a while. I think he knew."

"Knew what?"

"They sense things. They have instincts."

Lee swallowed another mouthful of coffee and studied his wife's face.

"This was a different dream than the others," Patty said. "Very different."

"In a good way, I hope."

"In every way."

"Was I in this one," Lee said.

He sipped and Patty sipped.

"No. Not this time. It was just me and the baby."

"Did something terrible happen. Because right now my head is pounding and I don't—"

"It's okay, Lee. The baby was with me," Patty said. "He was strapped in. He was fine." She stared into her coffee mug. "We were driving down Newport Avenue. We hit that intersection—you know that intersection right before you get to East Providence."

"Yes," Lee said.

"What's that street?"

"Which one?"

"The name of that street."

"Which street?" Lee said.

"The one that crosses over."

Lee waited until Patty looked up. "Pawtucket Avenue?"

"That one. We were there," Patty said. "At that intersection. A police cruiser was parked on the meridian. A patrolman had climbed on top of the hood to direct traffic. He had one of those orange flags and he was waving everyone to the right." Patty waved her fist in the air. "But no one was paying attention. They drove straight past."

"What did you do?"

"I turned of course. I turned right and drove fast and looked for a place to hide. But there were just houses, all those old houses we had looked at when we were ready to buy. Do you remember those houses?"

Lee nodded.

"And I could see the drivers pulling over and abandoning their cars, running across lawns and banging on doors, yelling for help."

"You still had the baby?"

"Yes."

"What did you do?"

"I kept going. I drove to that place, that storage center. Where you stored your mother's stuff for a while. I drove there. I found an empty unit and I took the baby inside, and I shut the door and we waited."

"How was the baby through all of this?"

"Oh, he was fine. He was sleeping. He didn't have a clue as to what was happening."

"What was happening," Lee said.

"I didn't know. I had no idea. I was huddled inside, holding the baby, and thinking about the policeman. I could hear people running past, a mix of wild voices. There was so much screaming, Lee. My ears still hurt. It was like dreaming in stereo. Every so often someone banged the door, but no way was I going to open it."

"So what did you do?"

"I held the baby and I rocked and I listened to the people outside. I was frightened, Lee. I didn't know what was happening."

"What was?"

"We weren't trapped. I didn't feel trapped. I was afraid for the baby, but I felt safe."

"Is that it? Is that the end of it?"

"No. God," Patty said. "There was this bang, loud." She sipped her coffee. "It shook me. I huddled with the baby against my breast and I covered his ears. I can still hear it."

"You can hear it now?"

Patty nodded. "The ring of it. The echo."

"What was it? Was it nuclear blast loud?"

"Worse, Lee. It was everything. The hard sound of the whole world weeping."

Lee looked suddenly down. He rocked on his feet.

"And then it wouldn't stop. I held the baby and I waited. My ears hurt. When the ringing stopped I thought I was deaf. There was nothing. No sound, Lee. I figured my eardrums had popped. I thought I was permanently deaf."

"Were you? In the dream, I mean?"

"I thought so, but then the baby popped his eyes open and he made a little sound."

Lee lifted his cup but didn't drink. "What kind of sound?"

"A baby sound, Lee. A gurgling. It's not important. It meant I wasn't deaf. It was the world that had gone quiet. Do you understand?"

"That's some dream," Lee said.

"So then I opened the door."

"There's more?"

"Bodies. They were everywhere. Lee. It was a horror. All intact, not a mark on them."

Lee moved his cup from one hand to the other. He looked at his wife. "So what did you do, Patty?"

"What could I do? I had the baby. So I started walking. I stepped around bodies, stepped over them. I got to the car, but there was no way I could drive with so many bodies in the road. So I walked, holding the baby high with his face against my breast so he wouldn't see any of it. I walked up Pawtucket Avenue to the intersection where the cop had been directing traffic. Then I walked down Newport Avenue, heading here."

"You were bringing the baby home?"

"Yes. All I wanted was to get home. I felt sure everything would be fine once I got home. But it was very hard walking."

"Because of the baby?"

"No, silly. Because of the bodies. I stepped over hundreds of bodies."

"Did you make it home?"

"Thank god I made it."

"And then?"

"And then I woke up."

"You didn't come in?"

"No."

"Why not?" said Lee.

"Because I woke up."

"What about me? I would have been in the house."

"I told you, you weren't in this one."

"But I was in the others. Where was I in this one?"

"I don't know, Lee."

"But I might have been in the house?"

Patty shrugged.

"Did you look? I mean, did you look?"

"I don't remember looking. I remember the house looked fine, and the baby acted fine."

"Was my car here?"

"Your car?"

"Yes. In the driveway. Didn't you wonder what might have happened to me?"

77

"Everybody was dead, Lee. Everybody. Just me and the baby survived."

"That's it? That's all?"

"Then the dog barked. I woke up. My heart was pounding."

Lee held his cup with both hands. He looked at Patty until she looked away.

"That's one bizarre dream. Wow. Did you write it down?"

Patty shook her head no.

"You should write it down," Lee said.

"I couldn't sleep after. I was awake for hours."

"You should have woke me," Lee said.

"Why?"

He lifted his cup. "I could have sat with you." He watched his wife lift her cup in both hands close to her chin.

She held the mug against her chin. "I sat a while in the baby's room."

"Oh Patty," Lee said. "Why didn't you wake me?"

"It was alright this time. Really. I stood in the doorway and that didn't feel so bad. I stayed there only a few minutes. Then I got a glass of water from the kitchen. The dog was so funny. He kept looking at me with his head tilted to one side. I'm sure he sensed something, because when I went back into the baby's room, he followed me. He followed me, Lee."

"He's just a dog," Lee said.

"I sat in there and tried to remember the baby's face but I couldn't remember it. That made me sad but I didn't cry. I thought I would. I think I started to, but then I focused my thoughts on some of the things we've talked about in group. You know. And then the room felt very soothing."

"Maybe you should stop now, save the rest for our next session," Lee said.

"I used the pump."

"Oh, Patty."

"I know. I know, Lee. And I'm sorry, I am. But they felt so full. I couldn't stand the ache. So I did one breast then the other. The dog sat with me the whole time, watching, then he followed me back to the kitchen. I poured the milk down the drain then I got him some water. I filled his dish."

Lee set his cup on the bedside table. He pressed a knee onto the bed and reached for the cup in his wife's hand. "He's just a dog, Patty.

78

A dumb little dog barking over an empty bowl. You can't keep reacting to every little thing."

Patty's eyes reflected sunlight. "I know, Lee," she said, "I'm not stupid. I know he's only a dog. I'm not talking about that. I'm talking about everything but that." She handed him her empty cup. "I think I'd like to visit the grave today."

"You do? I mean, okay. Sure. I'll make us some breakfast and then we'll go," Lee said. "If that's what you want."

"I do," Patty said.

The Significance of Sunlight

The rooming house—a three-story Colonial big as a church—was on the corner of Euclid Avenue and Thayer Street, in a bustling section of Providence's East Side, a tough spot to find parking so late in the afternoon. The woman who managed the place didn't live there. Her name was Lillian White and she lived in an apartment above her real estate office two streets over. On the phone, she had agreed to meet me on the wide wooden porch of Seven Euclid Avenue.

She showed me two rooms, one on the second floor, one on the third. They were furnished the same, carpeted with mismatched squares of rug remnants. Both had wallpaper that belonged in a funeral home. The third-floor room was smaller, with a single window cut into the sloped roof. The shared bath was filthy and the community kitchen a grimy mess. While I measured my height against the room's slanted ceiling, Mrs. White explained that the third floor was cheaper, so I said I'd take it.

She wouldn't accept a check, even with I.D., so I had to take a walk to find an ATM, pull out cash, then go back and pay the lady. She refused to take my money until I had read a list of rules and signed a piece of paper stating I had understood them. She penned a receipt and handed me a key for the room and another key for the downstairs door. After all of it was settled, I drove back toward home. If I hurried, I could still make dinner. That is, if Donna had found the energy to cook.

I drove Hope Street into Pawtucket and ran into a snarl of rush-hour traffic near Blackstone Boulevard. I witnessed two minor accidents. I sat behind a fuming truck and listened to a van blasting "Don't Let The Sun Catch You Crying." The van had tinted windows so I couldn't see inside. I tried to remember which group sang that song, then the truck roared its engine and started moving again.

The closer I got to familiar streets, the darker it became outside and the more my excitement wore down, until eventually it settled into concern. Not concern for Donna's ongoing battle with depression, because I was done with all that. My problem was more immediate: how to get out quickly, how to escape with mind and heart intact.

I wasn't taking anything from the marriage. The furniture, the wedding gifts, the photos ... she could have all that. I didn't want anything except what I'd come with.

I calculated the number of boxes I would need for my books and wondered if one liquor store would give me that many boxes. I imagined myself having to go from store to store, begging for boxes. I could use grocery bags for my clothes. How many bags, I wondered. My brain skipped into high gear and I missed the turn for my street.

I kept driving.

I rode around until almost midnight. I drove past my house twice. The windows were already dark, but I wanted to allow Donna plenty of time to fall asleep. I would tell her tomorrow, in the brightness of morning. I was doing the right thing, no question. After eighteen months, a clean, quick separation was the proper decision. Doing the right thing is always hardest during the spaces in between.

By the third pass, I was almost out of fuel. So I parked. I sat in the car a minute, then went inside. Donna was sitting in the dark smoking a cigarette. The tip glowed red, then faded to crossing-guard orange. I could smell the smoke but couldn't see it. I pulled the string on the overhead light. She was still wearing the bathrobe she'd put on that morning. Her hair was wild.

I didn't hesitate. I pulled a breath and told her I had found a place, a single room. "It's not much to look at, but it's affordable," I said.

She dropped her cigarette into a soda can, then jerked her hand up to her face so fast I thought she meant to slap herself. She touched her chin. She worked the tips of her fingers into the flesh beneath her mouth. Her lips trembled.

"I have to share a bathroom and a kitchen with six other tenants, but that should be all right. We'll see. It's small. But it's furnished. A bed. A chair. There's a little table that could be used as a desk." I shrugged. "It's on the third floor. I didn't want the third, but it was twenty bucks cheaper. The second floor is cleaner. The bathroom especially. But not much cleaner. Not twenty dollars' worth. I imagine I'll get used to the stairs. Maybe they'll get me to quit smoking. I have a window that faces east, but there's not much of a view. Just a parking lot. Still, I'll get sunlight in the morning. I'll wake up every day to sunlight."

I held my smile and tried to appear upbeat. The smile came easy and I could have held it longer except that Donna began to sob behind her hand, which I didn't realize until her arm started trembling. I reached for her, but she turned away.

So I gave her a minute.

Sometimes with Donna a minute was all it took, a moment to digest, to put matters in perspective and push dark thoughts aside. In her better moments she sometimes pulled it off. I gave her a good solid minute to pull it off now.

Would anyone believe I was rooting for her?

When her minute was up, I brought out the keys to my new home and put them on the table. Donna looked at them like she'd never seen keys before. She seemed to be having trouble drawing breath.

"Oh god," she gasped. "I need to lie down. I can't deal with this right now. I can't."

Her voice trembled like a song fading in and out, a familiar song, caught between stations.

Treasure Hunt

One day toward the end, Bobo brought home a game in a bottle. Big black bottle like a magnum of champagne. He tried sneaking it in behind his back, but I saw the foil neck. I saw that shine and knew what it was, and I figured we were celebrating. I thought Bobo had tossed in the towel on all that A.A. gunk and we were finally getting back to our lives.

"What are you hiding?" I said, sitting bolt-right.

Bobo looked sharp, handsome as a soldier in his neat doorman's outfit.

"Nothing. Not a thing," he said, beaming like it was Christmas.

My heart started going. I pushed into my slippers and padded across the linoleum. I felt bad about my housecoat and my hair. I pushed up on tip toe and kissed Bobo's cheek. His face felt warm. I figured he'd already had a taste.

"Close your eyes," Bobo said, but it was already too late for that.

"Oh, Bobo," I said, as he brought the bottle around.

"Go on. Take it," he said.

I held my hands apart shaking like a crazy girl trying to measure something.

"Go on," he said.

Soon as I touched it I knew. "It's fake," I said. "It's plastic." The thing had no weight. I shook it hard and it made a sound like a jar full of pennies.

"It's a game," Bobo said. "Look inside."

I handed the bottle to him and shuffled back to the couch.

"One or two players," Bobo said.

I kicked off my slippers and pushed my feet beneath the afghan. I couldn't even look at him.

"Says so right here. One or two players."

Christ, I thought, he just doesn't get it.

"I thought maybe you could play while I'm at work. Help you pass the time," said Bobo.

I dug out the remote from between the cushions. I said, "Thank you very much but time doesn't need any help passing around here."

I pointed and clicked, flipping channels.

"And I don't like surprises. Especially joke gifts."

"Jesus, Annie. I thought it was a riot. I thought it would make you smile. Christ," he said, "I almost bought two of them."

83

I couldn't look at him for fear of seeing that damn A.A. pin that he wore like a badge.

"Okay. Alright. Tell you what," Bobo said. "You don't like surprise gifts. Fine. Not a problem. I'll sell it to you. I'll sell you this game in a bottle for a smile. Half a smile," Bobo said.

I thought: God, please hide from me the kitchen knives.

Lately, Bobo's one year pin was a constant reminder. It had been nearly fourteen months now. Always hoping, never getting. Every day waiting for some part of something to change. It wasn't the booze. I never drank like Bobo. And the few times I did I never did anyone any harm. Most nights I had been the driver, the one who always got us home. It wasn't all the dumb meetings, or the new people, half of whom were nuts. Though I still missed some of the old gang, the good souls. And the colored lights, and the music. More than anything I missed that wild dizzy feeling I'd get when Bobo picked me up and twirled me around the dance floor.

"Some guy was selling them out of his car," Bobo said. "Old VW, trunk in the front. Spider crack on the passenger side, but the body was mint. I told him it could use a paint job. I said Sir, I'll scrape her down and prime her for twenty bucks and half your inventory. I was serious. He had some jewelry, a lot of silver. A few pieces of gold. And all these here games. I'll fix that windshield, too, I said. But he wasn't buying, he was selling."

I huffed my breath, tapping the remote until I hit one of my stories.

"You know what it is?" Bobo said. "You know what I think it is? People see this uniform, they figure I'm a cop."

I crossed my arms and ground my teeth at the TV.

"Hey. I got a really nice tip today."

"Shush!" I said.

That shut him up. Bobo had learned to respect my day time shows.

Then he said, "Well, what did you think, Annie? What in hell did you think?"

But I just let that go.

I don't know how long I sat with my chin pointed at the TV, how long I waited for the heat to leave my face. I didn't know what channel I was watching. When I finally focused again, I saw a woman's hand slide a silver revolver from a black purse. Then the picture faded. Then a lady standing in a pond beside a white unicorn held up a bar of green soap. I muted the set.

84

I picked at my fingernails, but I really had no choice but to look over at Bobo.

By then he'd unscrewed the bottom of the bottle and was staring into it, holding the thing like a bouquet of flowers. I watched him try and fit his hand in, but he couldn't get past the knuckles. He used two fingers to pluck out some loose playing cards and a cellophane bag of colored pieces. He dropped them on the table then stuck his nose in like he meant to get a good whiff of whatever else was in there.

Who knows what he was looking at.

The commercial was over, but I didn't care about that. I watched Bobo turn the bottle over and slap the side until a curved booklet slid part way out.

"Here we go," he said, grinning at me, like he'd just found the answer to what we were doing, the two of us, living in a cramped three-room apartment overlooking a filthy river.

Bobo sat down to study what he'd found and I did what I normally do when I feel one of my headaches coming on. I closed my eyes and pretended I was some place else.

I had a short dream of the river, black as a road, and so full of chemicals that on rainy days soap suds flew up past the windows. I dreamed it was winter, and suds were flying, and the world outside was flurrying snow both ways.

When I opened my eyes, Bobo had the game set up on top of the coffee table. There was a cloth map with oceans and islands in bright blues, yellows and reds. Wavy dashed lines connected the islands. In one corner a starred compass showed us North.

I blinked at Bobo. He put on one of his ain't-life-wonderful smiles and held up one of the playing pieces—a tiny green ship with curved sails. He moved it in front of my face as if the ship were climbing and falling, drifting on a turbulent sea.

"Want to play now?" he asked. "I think I got it figured out."

I shot him a look like he'd just sprouted a third eye.

"Aren't you supposed to be at a meeting?" I said.

He put the little ship down. "Nope. No meeting tonight." He had his nose in the little book.

"Wednesday, isn't it?" I said.

He pretended to read, flipping pages. He looked like an idiot sitting there with his doorman's jacket on; all the braids and embroidered swirls made him look like a crazy admiral plotting a war.

"So why no meeting," I said.

"Hmm?"

I picked up a red ship, the exact color of my nail polish. I made a fist and squeezed until it cut into my flesh.

"Thought Wednesday was commitment night," I said.

"It is," Bobo said, "but I'm not going."

He flipped another page, but I saw his eyes tilt up. "The group is going over to the ACI. I told 'em I'd pass. It's not a crime to miss one here and there."

"You'd know better than me," I said.

The ACI was the Adult Correctional Institute, a local prison where Bobo's A.A. group sometimes went to counsel inmates with substance abuse problems. I knew why Bobo wasn't going. Some years before, he'd done nine months in a similar type of facility for beating a store clerk who refused to give him change. Bobo's ex had a restraining order against him and he'd been up forty-eight hours straight plotting how to kill her and kidnap his daughter and get away with it. When the clerk told him he wasn't in the change business, Bobo had beat the man half to death with a sausage of semi-frozen cookie dough. It wasn't something he was proud of.

"I think you should go to your meeting," I said.

I dropped the tiny ship in the pocket of my housecoat hoping that might screw up the game somehow.

Bobo watched me do it. He said, "Maybe you want to go with me?"

"Ha ha," I said, and picked up the fake bottle. I read the label: TREASURE HUNT. An adventure game for adults. I said, "Not much of a commitment if you don't go."

Bobo shrugged. "Here's what you do," he said.

He picked up a card with a treasure chest printed on it. All the cards had them. Tiny chests heaped with cutouts of cellophane and foil. He flipped this one over and read: "Set course South by South-East and roll again."

He pulled at his lower lip with two of his fingers.

He looked at me as if the card meant something.

"Not like you to miss a meeting," I said.

"I've missed before," Bobo said.

I pulled my sleeve back and looked at my wrist as though a watch were there. "You can still make it. Not too late." Then I stood up and turned my back on Bobo. "I thought AA was all about helping people."

"It is," he said.

"Well, you're sure not helping anyone around here."

I went into the kitchen. The floor was cold. I heard Bobo's shoes squeak the linoleum, but I opened the refrigerator anyway, leaning in, pretending I had no idea he was right behind me.

"What did you do today?" he said.

I moved an egg carton from one shelf to another. I shoved a jug of spring water to one side. I tried to make it look like I was searching. But there wasn't much to look at.

"Do you want some eggs?" I said.

"No. I want you to look at me."

"I don't know if there's bread. Maybe you can go for some."

"Annie, look at me. Look at me, baby."

I took a jar of mayonnaise from the door rack. My hand was shaking, my whole arm. I held the jar in both hands and picked at the label. Bobo put his hand on my shoulder. "Let's go out," he said, turning me. "We'll get Chinese. I got a nice tip today." He gave me a little squeeze, pulling, like he was trying to lift me. "What do you say? We'll squander the rent money."

I started peeling the label from the jar. I shook my head real slow. "I'd have to get dressed," I said. "I'd have to shower and wash my hair, put on makeup. Iron. I don't want to do all that."

"Okay," Bobo said. "We'll get it to go, then. We'll have a party right here."

I let him take the mayonnaise jar. He put it in the refrigerator and closed the door. "Egg rolls, fried rice, some of those lobster things you like. Huh?"

I shrugged.

"Sure," Bobo said. "We'll get chop sticks, a whole bag of fortune cookies, the works."

I nodded, hugging myself while Bobo hugged me, too.

"Great," Bobo said, letting go. "Super," he said. He took his keys off the counter and jingled them in front of my face. "You get cozy. Your hair looks fine. Don't change nothing. I'll be back in a jiffy." He bent his knees and kissed my forehead. I knew what came next. I hated saying it now.

"God, I love you," he said.

I swallowed. "I love you, too," I said.

And I gave him a little smile so he'd think everything was all peaches and cream.

"Sure. See. There you go," Bobo said. "There's the face I love."

87

I leaned against the refrigerator and listened to his thumps on the stairs. It sounded like he was running. I heard the downstairs door, then I went to the window and waited for him to appear from beneath the canopy. He came out twirling, dodging traffic to get to his car, and then he spun again, waving wildly. I stepped back, and held my breath. Then I felt bad and I pressed my hand to the glass, but it was too late.

I stayed at the window for a while, watching the traffic. Then I went back in and knelt by the coffee table to clear a spot for us to eat. I held up the bottle by its neck and began dropping things into the bottom: ships, playing cards, instruction booklet. I folded up the map and stuffed that in there, too. Then I screwed the bottom on tight and held the bottle against my chest. I carried it over to the couch that way.

I flicked past all the news and then a couple of game shows. I watched part of a cartoon with a cartoon mouse tricking a cartoon cat. I held the bottle the whole time, rocking slowly back and forth. I found a channel with people I recognized, faces I knew. It was an old black and white movie. I watched five or ten minutes of that, then I pushed the bottle lower. I held it between my thighs, tilting the neck up, careful not to shake it. I twisted the top to see if that came off, but it didn't. I remembered the way champagne used to tickle my nose, the bubbles popping, and that first slippery taste on the back of my tongue. I thought about Bobo picking me up, and everybody making a circle around us while he swung me and swung me like I had no weight. Like I was just something in orbit and he was my sun.

During a hand cream commercial I twisted around and got to my knees. I pressed my forehead to the glass and stared down at the heart-stopping cold water that Bobo said ran half a mile deep in spots. I wondered if he had been lying when he said his father had once caught fish from the bridge using nothing but worms on a string. I watched the water and decided if there were any fish still down there, they'd be eyeless, bloated creatures surviving on garbage and soap suds.

I tugged the afghan up to my chin, and I did what I always do when I feel like I'm falling. I closed my eyes and waited for Bobo to catch me.

Wager

I'm in this story, though only because I have to be. I've taken liberties to keep my appearance to the barest minimum. The important people are Tony and Phil. You'll need to excuse Phil. He's a wreck, jittery from lack of sleep and too much coffee. Overwhelmed by uncommon circumstances, he hasn't bathed, shaved or eaten since Thursday's late afternoon breakfast, when he was chewing on a slice of rubbery bacon, commenting to Tony, his roommate and life partner, how premium quality, center-cut bacon really should never be cooked on a paper towel in a microwave.

That's when the phone rang and Phil answered.

The caller's voice was flat, cold, nonchalant to the point of sounding breezy. It was a voice right out of a Hitchcock thriller, the moment right before some woman screams. After a rather brief, one-sided conversation full of numerous ugly and melodramatic references to shattered bones, torn flesh, broken teeth, the caller said, "Imagine how it's going to feel to have both your eyes scooped out with a soup spoon?"

"Is this about the money," Phil asked.

"Yeah," replied the caller. "It's about the money."

That was Thursday. Now it's Sunday, and very simply what will happen is sometime before midnight two men will arrive and cut off two of Phil's fingers—one finger for each IOU that Phil has defaulted on.

Phil is a much better piano player than he is a gambler. Playing piano is how he earns his living, affording him and Tony a low-key, cozy existence these last few years, except lately things have been slow.

At half-past eight Tony dragged an old suitcase from the storage closet and rifled through it. He changed into a black leather skirt and a crisp white blouse. He strapped on chunky open-toe heels, fixed his hair, put on makeup, then sat down to wait.

For an hour he waited, and that's how we find him, now, still waiting. His legs are clean shaven and bare. Even in winter, Nevada nights are sticky, much too humid for stockings.

He walks quickly across the hardwood, passing Phil, clacking his heels on purpose, hyped by having to sit, chain smoking, fully made up for the last hour, listening to Phil dialing, hearing Phil's pathetic speeches, then the long horrible silences between the sniffling sobs Phil makes while waiting for the phone to ring.

Tony sits at a mahogany vanity, an heirloom from his mother, and uses a small brush to highlight his eyes. At twenty-three he is exactly half Phil's age but appears even younger with the sharp cheekbones and long thin frame of an adolescent girl. He studies his reflection and practices his smile. His make-up is already so precise the colors appear carved.

"Wipe that pitiful look off your face," he says to Phil, who walks in, shoulders slumped, shaking his head at the floor.

"One of them still might call. It's earlier there."

"Forget them," Tony says. "Anyone going to call would have."

"Who do you mean," Phil says.

"Any of them. All of them. Jesus, Phil," Tony says and sighs. "Just forget it, Phil," he says, leaning toward his reflection. "The cavalry is not coming."

Phil is a large man with beefy arms and enormous hands, somewhat of a joke for a piano player, and hulking shoulders nearly as wide as Tony's vanity bench. He puts his big hands on the wing-like bones of Tony's shoulders.

"Wait thirty minutes. Please."

"Don't start up again," Tony says, slowly tracing the thin arch of an eyebrow he penciled in an hour earlier.

"I have a bad feeling," Phil says. His gaze is in the mirror as his fingers press into the flesh of Tony's neck.

Tony's reflection frowns back.

"That's not helping," Tony says, shrugging him off, but Phil's grip remains firm. Tony stops all activity until Phil lifts his hands away.

"I'm sorry. My nerves are raw," Phil says. "I'm not thinking straight."

"Well, relax. It's almost over."

"It's not over. How can you say it's over."

"I said almost. Don't worry. I'll get the money."

"Forget the money. Now it's this. How the hell can I relax? It's everything now."

"Nothing bad will happen."

"You could get arrested," Phil says. "That would be bad. Or worse. You could pick up a nut. Some psychopath. The world is a horror."

"Tell me about it," Tony says. "I made my living this way, remember?"

"I remember," Phil says.

"Never got a psychopath. Millionaires, politicians, movie actors, a couple of novelists, men with power, men with brains. Those I got, and plenty of them."

"I know," Phil says. "Let's not talk about it."

"I've played daddy's princess and I've played daddy's whore so don't lecture me about the horrors of the world. Okay? I'm a polished professional."

"I know. I know all that."

Tony winks, flashes a winning smile, then pouts and uses a thin pencil to darken the outline of his lips. "So, big deal. I'm back for one night. Call it my encore. My grand finale." He shakes his hair which is jet black, straight and thick, cropped one length at the shoulders, center parted. His hair rises as it twirls. He licks his teeth, emits a low, throaty growl as he gives his shoulders a little shake. "Watch out boys, Cleopatra reporting for night patrol."

He uses the pencil to scrawl a number on the glass. "That the total?"

Phil stares then nods.

"That's the whole bundle? You're sure? Including all their crazy interest?"

Phil looks at his feet and says. "Let me make one more call before you go. I've got this guy in Pittsburgh. He owes me his life."

"Don't be a fool," Tony says.

"We've still got four hours."

"Less than four. Get real, Phil."

"There's still time."

"You don't know. They could be outside that door right now."

"I've thought of that," Phil says.

"They could be anywhere, listening to every word we say."

"I've thought of that too," Phil says, looking at the door. "Let me make this call. Last one. The guy could wire us the money. We'd have it within the hour."

"Stop embarrassing yourself."

"There's still my mother."

"You can not call your mother," Tony says.

"Okay. Your father, then? What about him?"

"My father?"

"You could say its a medical emergency. That you need an operation."

"Oh, that'll work. He'll think I'm having it nipped and tucked, sliced and inverted. Finally, the daughter he never had. Please dial that number for me," Tony says, then blots his lips with a tissue as he studies the mirror. "Are you crying again? Phil? Tilt your chin up, please. Oh, Good lord. One giant step back. Go. Move. This blouse is silk. Do you know what tears do to silk?"

"I'm sorry," Phil says, sniffling.

"You're starting again."

"I know."

"Don't start, Philip. Not now. I've got to go to work. Take a pill or something."

"I took a pill."

"Then have a drink. Have a couple of drinks. Look at me. Focus. This is important."

Phil sniffs, "What?"

Tony pinches Phil's chin, directs his gaze. "It's simple. I'll go, and in a few hours I'll come back. I'll have the money. You'll pay what you owe. Then we'll forget I did this. Am I right?"

Phil nods.

"You'll pay and that will be the end of it. Then no more. You understand? You can't keep doing this."

Phil nods and paces while Tony inventories his purse.

"No more living like two rats in a cage. I should have done this days ago."

"They can have my fingers," Phil says. "As many as they want."

"What's that, Phil?"

"I said that's a lot of money in a few hours."

"That's not what you said."

"That's what I'm saying now."

"What are you saying?"

"I'm saying it's a lot of money for a few hours work."

Tony glares at the mirror, gets eye contact, blows a kiss at Phil who is tapping a tight fist against his thigh.

"How do I look," Tony says, doing modeling turns.

The corners of Phil's mouth extend then retract.

"Am I hot or am I hot?"

"You're lovely," Phil says.

"But am I hot? I need to hear I'm hot."

"You look very beautiful," Phil says.

Tony smirks. "Good enough." He snaps the purse shut. "I'll call when I've got the cash."

Phil nods, eyes averted, chin down. He keeps nodding all the way to the door. He watches Tony unhook the chain and slide back the bolt.

"Kiss for luck," Tony says, offering his cheek.

Phil leans, but hardly.

"Tony? I'm sorry about this."

"I know, Phil."

"This whole ugly mess," Phil says, and sighs. "You ever feel like your life is on one side of the room and you're handcuffed to a chair on the other?"

"All the time," Tony says and tilts his head so that a curtain of hair slides between him and Phil. He holds the pose until Phil reaches up, sweeps the hair aside, finds Tony showing his perfect teeth. He kisses Phil's knuckle, then digs deep into his purse. "Here. Hold on to this until I see you again."

"What is that? What are you giving me—a gun?"

"Take it, Phil. I have to go."

Phil holds the pistol upside-down, pinched between his thumb and index finger. "Where did you get this?"

"I bought it."

"When?"

"What difference does it make?"

"For what?"

"Phil, please. Do me a favor. Shut up, and listen. I want you to understand something. For the record. Just in case, okay?"

"In case of …?"

"In case anything should prevent me from getting back here in time. In case I'm not the hot shot hustler I used to be. Okay? I want you to know that right up until the exact moment you came into my life, I never thought I could care about anyone more than myself. I mean that, Philip. I adore you more than life itself. So you hold onto that thought, okay? And don't be afraid to point that gun at anyone who shows up at the door. Okay? Because you're right about the world being a nasty place. It's a sewer. And no one can predict what might happen to anyone going down into its mucky bottom."

Phil's nerves are shot. His hands tremble as he rights the gun, cocks the piece, stares at Tony, then aims the pistol at his right temple.

"It's not loaded," Tony says.

"But if it were," Phil says. "If it were."

Knock, knock.

And that's where I come in, me and my partner, like the punch line of a joke nobody wants to hear.

Newborn

I'll sometimes tell a story, not because it's very interesting or insightful, but merely to get rid of it. That's all this is: An eradication, a flushing out of sorts. I'm constantly attempting to decontaminate my consciousness.

One time when I was fifteen I found a baby in a dumpster. I kid you not. I'm being sincere. But don't worry, the kid wasn't dead or anything, so this is not one of those gruesome dead-baby-found-in-a-dumpster stories. The gruesome part, if there is one, concerns my father, Robert Alan Thurber Senior, PFC, US Marine Corps, whom, in the summer of '69, was well on his way to becoming another American casualty of the Vietnam War. But this story isn't really about him either.

The night I found the kid in the dumpster was pretty hot, though probably not quite Vietnam jungle hot. While my father was crouched in some rice paddy dodging sniper fire I was behind the Howard Johnson's restaurant and motor lodge in Pawtucket, right off the exit ramp. I lived across the street with my mother and sister in a cramped three-room apartment overlooking an EZ-off/EZ-on gas station. Though I was too young to be legally employed, nights and weekends I worked at HoJo's as a dishwasher.

That Saturday, around midnight, I was hauling trash from a banquet, and as I tossed garbage bags into the dumpster I heard a sort of wailing. I followed the sound, climbed half inside, felt something wrapped in a sheet and peeled it open.

I didn't expect to see a baby. A puppy or a kitten, maybe.

It was smaller than my sister's Chatty Kathy doll, raw and pink, with a stump of umbilical cord still attached. I held it at arms length for a few seconds but it wouldn't stop crying so I gently placed it atop a bag of garbage and went inside.

Andrea, one of the waitresses, was in the break room sorting her tips and stacking coins in columns. I asked where the manager was.

"Who knows," she said and shrugged.

The manager was a squat, pudgy man with thinning hair. His name was Mr. Silva and he had gone to high school with my mother, which is how I got the dishwashing job in the first place.

I found Silva in his little office, a room that measured four-feet by six-feet and contained nothing but a desk, a chair, a 3-drawer filing cabinet, and another chair for visitors. The visitors' seat was a cheap folding chair and I barely got it open before I sat down. I felt suddenly dizzy.

Silva was writing on a clipboard. "What?" he said.

I gulped air and swallowed hard.

"There's a baby in the dumpster," I said.

Silva kept writing. "A baby what?"

I shrugged, thinking he meant boy or girl. "I didn't look."

He stopped writing and looked at me above his glasses. "You didn't look? So how do you know what you saw?"

My knees were trembling so I put a hand on each of them. "It was wrapped in a bed-sheet. Looks pretty new. It's not wearing a diaper."

Silva's face changed in shape in color. "Show me," he said.

We walked past the break room where Andrea was still counting her tips.

"Hey, Silva. We need to talk," she shouted.

"Not now," Silva said.

"I want to up my hours. I'm not making it on four shifts a week."

"Not now," Silva said.

As we stepped outside, I listened for the baby, but there was no sound except the whoosh of traffic on the freeway. I began to wonder if I had seen what I thought I saw.

Silva walked up close to the dumpster and stuck his head through the opening.

"Holy shit," he said.

"What did I tell you," I said.

Andrea bumped up behind me. "Hey, Silva," she said.

She squeezed past me, took a few steps, then stopped.

For a moment she blocked my view, then I saw Silva walking towards us with the baby in his arms.

"Where in god's name did that come from," Andrea said.

Because I was paid cash "under the table" or "off the books," I wasn't legally an employee of Howard Johnson's Corporation, so when the police came, Silva told them he found the kid.

The next day his name and picture were in the newspaper.

The article said the police delivered the baby to Pawtucket Memorial Hospital where doctors reported it to be in good health. Hospital staff nicknamed him "Luke," short for "Lucky." They described Luke as, male, Caucasian, 17 inches long, 6 pounds, 9 ounces.

A week later, a local church threw Silva a dinner where he was presented with a plaque and praised as a hero. Within a month HoJo's promoted him from restaurant manager to general director of the motor lodge.

Bad news for me.

Silva's replacement was the former banquet coordinator, a woman named Vera, a strict-librarian type who did everything by the book. When I showed up for my shift Vera pulled me into her tiny office and told me I was a valued member of the team and a hard worker. She invited me to reapply when I turned sixteen.

In short: she fired me, even though I didn't legally work there.

I never saw Mr. Silva again, though I ran into Andrea the waitress a few years later at a bus stop. This was right after I had gotten married and my wife was expecting our first child, though I didn't mention any of that to Andrea.

She remembered my name. We made small talk until her bus came. Before she got onboard, she said, "Hey. how about that night Silva found a baby in the dumpster. Wasn't that something?"

I said I remembered hearing about the incident but I wasn't working that night.

"You weren't?" she said, "Oh, sorry, sweetie. I must have you mixed up with another dishwasher."

From the steps of the bus she blew a kiss off her fingertips. I pretended to catch it in my fist like I would a flipped coin, all the time wishing she hadn't mentioned Silva or the baby.

I never told anyone it was me who found the kid.

Luke. Lucky. Whoever.

One summer, six or seven years before the dumpster incident, my sister found a newborn bird that had fallen from its nest. The thing was featherless, raw looking. She wanted to put it back, but we couldn't find any nest in the overhanging trees even though we climbed every one looking. Finally, she scooped the bird into a coffee can, carried it over to the church and left it on the front steps. She claimed God would take care of it, that it was officially His bird now, but I didn't believe that for a second, because whose goddamn bird was it in the first place?

Same with my father. Whose war was he fighting? Not mine. Not yours. Another thick-headed, gung-ho Marine, who believed he was humping through hell in order to save the world from the spread of communism.

Don't get me wrong. I'm pushing sixty and though I never went to war I still believe in god and country. I know where the country is. Right beneath my feet. But where the fuck is god when you need him.

Moon Time

You won't remember this until your own mother dies.

It's August, after midnight, the house so quiet the darkness hums. You're eight years old, standing barefoot on a chair by the stove in your dead grandmother's kitchen. You can't recall ever being up this late. But you're on a mission—fixing hot cocoa for your sister who is upstairs, bleeding to death. She's twelve and thin. She won't last long, so you're in somewhat of a hurry, heating milk in a saucepan, stirring with a wooden spoon. When the surface breaks into tiny bubbles, you pour in the cocoa powder, swirling the clumps toward the center. Beneath the stove's hood-lamp the milk turns muddy brown.

You lower the flame, dump in the sugar. Grandma's recipe is precise: one cup of cocoa, one cup of sugar, a long simmer and a slow, constant stir.

Though she is dead and buried, you feel her presence more than you did in the funeral parlor. She's guiding your hand, telling you again, "Simmer. Never boil. Watch the flame. Keep a constant stir. That's how you mix the love in."

Your arm feels numb as wood. Her instructions prevent you from nodding off and catching the sleeve of your pajamas on fire.

You stir until her voice urges, "Enough. "

Your shoulders jerk and for a second you're startled to find yourself not in bed.

Though your parents insist this is your home now, how could it ever be anything but grandma's kitchen, grandma's house? Her cough drop and lemon smell remain in the carpet, in the upholstered furniture, in the dank air you swallow in sleep. All your mother's cleaning has failed. Despite hours of wide-open windows, and a heavy dose of chemical detergents, the old woman's scent remains.

Though your father has emptied closets, bagged and hauled away tons of junk, repainted ceilings and walls—every night the smell of grandma seeps back in.

Walking like you're balanced on a high wire, the cup and saucer clinks and rattles. You steady it with both hands through the doorway, into the hall. Your mother's shadow stretches and folds over the stairs. She's at the top, her hair wrapped in curlers. You can't see her face, but you expect she's angry.

You climb anyway, eyes on the steaming cup. The more you try to balance, the more cocoa laps the edges. A wave spills over, scolding your knuckle, but you manage to hold on.

Your mother descends. "What are you doing up? What is that?"

"Cocoa."

"Why are you drinking Cocoa? It's after midnight."

"It's for Mandy. To make her feel better."

"Stop. Freeze," says Mama, pinching the saucer.

Steam floats up between your faces.

"Let go. I've got it," she says.

But you don't release your grip. "I made it special. Grandma's way."

Your mother's forehead becomes a nest of lines as she lifts the cup away then sets it down one stair above. She manages this without spilling a drop.

"Sit," she says, patting a stair.

The two of you settle. You watch your mother's hands as she smooths the front of her nightgown.

"This is about the blood, isn't it? You're worried about the blood." Her eyes shine. "Do you know what puberty is?"

You shrug and press your knees together

"Okay," Mama says, "All right." She clears her throat, talks for a minute straight, speaking rapidly, slowing down only to stress the syllables of certain words. When she says "ovaries" and "menstruation," her chest moves noticeably with her breathing.

You nod each time she nods but you don't understand. You're thinking about the hot chocolate sitting there growing cold.

Finally, using one finger to sweep bangs from your eyes, she sums up, "All that's happened is Mandy's changing from a child's body into a young woman."

You nod again.

"The blood isn't a bad thing. It's a very good sign. It means Mandy is healthy and her body is working properly." One side of her mouth trembles and the last thing you expect is a smile. "God, I didn't get mine until I was almost fifteen. I was so scared. I didn't tell anyone." Her smile tapers off. "But your grandmother was no dummy. She figured it out the next time she did my laundry. Then she baked me a cake."

"A cake?"

"Chocolate, with fudge frosting. We had a regular celebration, just her and me. Then we talked a little about what to do the next time my period came. I remember she called it the Moon Time, because the word menstruation comes from Greek, meaning moon and power."

Mama's eyes close like she's falling asleep. She grips her knees, rocks gently forward, then uses the railing to pull herself up. "Mandy's back in bed. You get there too."

You tilt your head up. "What about the cocoa?"

Mama lifts cup and saucer, and starts down. "Don't worry about it."

You stand to watch her go. "Night, mama."

"Goodnight, sweetheart."

You marvel at the way your mother's shadow bends and glides over furniture. You wait more than a minute before creeping down to peek, finding your mom standing rigid with her back against the sink, the cup inches from her lips.

Her mouth twists suddenly, unleashing a whimper that steadily builds. She clamps a hand over her mouth as she bends, muffling her wail, folding as she collapses. You see aguish you cannot understand. Did you mix it wrong, not stir long enough?

You won't remember this night or your sister's blood or your mother's grief for years, not until the pastor leans in, his gentle hand on your elbow, bending awkwardly as though to sniff your neck, asking if there's anything special you wish to add to the eulogy, any tribute to your mother's life?

And it's then you remember—just the edges, the brittle parts, fleeting as a half forgotten dream—the rest too hokey, too sentimental, too precious to share.

Not Making Excuses

Call it happenstance. Simple dumb luck. Somebody went to jail. Then his replacement got shot. The people in charge needed a local guy. My name came up. Next thing I know I'm being met by that rare opportunity. Quick and easy work. Sweet payoff. The whole deal masterfully organized.: maps, timetables, meetings, a couple of dress rehearsals. All of it fully financed with no skimp. I even got an envelope of cash up front. "Walking around money," the man called it. "For living expenses. Don't go blowing it on whores and booze." He was a huge man, a giant with a gentle voice, a soft-spoken gorilla in a fine silk suit.

Naturally, I can't say who I was working with, or what we were after, or even how it all turned out. Specific details are never a good thing. What I can tell you is this: there were four of us—three no-nonsense professionals plus myself—and on this rainy, chilly November morning we had run into a last minute snag.

A little before six a.m., just a few hours before I was scheduled to meet up with my new business partners, I woke to the screech of tires. I cringed at the noise. It sounded not only ugly but far too familiar. It gave me belly flops and a pain in my head. So I looked out my second-story window to discover—well, nothing. Where I'd parked my car was now an empty space. Some low life had hot-wired my 1967 Pontiac Firebird, the finest automobile I'd ever owned, and driven off to god knows where.

Suffice it to say this untimely turn of events seriously complicated matters. Not only did the theft ruin my morning, but it threatened to nullify all subsequent mornings. My new associates were uncomplicated individuals. They had built a solid reputation for getting things done, no excuses. On this particular morning they required transportation, and it remained my personal responsibility to supply a legally registered vehicle with a little pep.

As usual I had no time, no budget, and too many promises dangling. I was nobody, just a jittery guy with a fast car and a talent for diversionary driving. So after a number of brief and disappointing phone calls, I set out walking. I went four miles through drizzling early-morning rain to where I knew I could find reliable, turbo-charged transportation.

But nothing ever goes easy for me.

Nina's Mustang wasn't on the street so I scaled the fence to see if she had hidden the car in the side yard. Nina was a lot better worrier than she was a wife. Whenever she fell behind a few payments she got super paranoid about the repo man creeping up on her precious car in the middle of the night. I hadn't talked to her in weeks, hadn't sent her a dime in months.

Between the abandoned brick building next door and our clapboard tenement house was a dumpster area with a dirt driveway boxed in by a high chain-link fence. The padlocked gate had a weave of vinyl slats so people couldn't peek inside. I climbed careful and slow because all the metal was slick with rain; plus I was dirt sober and less than steady on my feet. I tore the elbow patch of my sports jacket going over—all for nothing. The stupid car wasn't back there.

I continued walking around to the back, frowning at all the junk piled up. It was worse than when I'd lived here, There had obviously been a fire because there were fresh plywood boards nailed to the first floor windows and each window was surrounded by scorch marks stretching upward like the blackened fingerprints of a giant, and the whole place smelled like a dirty chimney.

Beside a stack of gray and rotting firewood was a dog on a chain sleeping with his mouth open. Not a very big animal but even so the beast didn't know me, so I climbed a garbage can beneath a fire escape and pulled myself up the ladder and in through a window to the second floor landing.

It was barely eight o'clock and already the people in 2D were frying onions and garlic. Somebody in 2C was singing in Spanish. The door on 2B was wide open; the place vacant, bare, and reeking of disinfectant. I dug out a key that had worn a bare spot in my wallet and let myself into 2A. Two things hit me in a heartbeat; the scent of Nina's cheap perfume, and the fact that there was a man in there. I heard him snoring before I even got the key out of the lock—he was louder than a rusty gate in a windstorm.

The sound echoed through the three rooms and for a moment I considered that it might be the TV because I could see the TV through the doorways of both rooms. Though, these snores didn't sound like TV noise. They sounded like a real man. So I walked through one room and stopped and leaned my head into the bedroom. Sure enough, there he was—a big fellow.

I held on to the door frame, listening to him wheeze and snort. He had a lot of snarly red hair, a wild beard with a wacky moustache—a huge viking of a man with a chest like matted fur. He was wearing white boxers and black crew socks, nothing else. I stepped inside and stood between the bed and the TV. The TV was showing cartoons with the sound all the way down. On the bed, the red haired man, a Viking giant, was making all the noise, an awful racket for just one man.

I crossed my arms and looked at the TV. I watched a cartoon cat chase a cartoon mouse with a broom, then with a shot-gun, then with a military jeep, then with a fire engine. I frowned at the man in the bed and thought about where I could get a gun—a small pistol would do—and how long it would take for me to go and make that deal, then get back here, all using public transportation.

I touched the power button on the TV and the picture popped. I leaned over the bed. The man's cheeks and forehead were pockmarked and freckled. His lips sputtered a little with each exhale. I held my breath and wondered if he wasn't playing a joke, pretending to snore like that.

Then I went to work. I kept an eye on him the whole time, watched in the dresser mirror as I moved across the room. I found a duffle bag on the floor of the closet and started throwing things in. There wasn't much I could find that belonged to me, but I didn't care. The duffle bag wasn't mine.

Both sides of the closet were filled with new clothes, new colors, new fabrics, dresses and blouses with tags still on them. I didn't waste my time with them. I checked the dresser. Someone had switched all the drawers around, rearranged everything. There was a lot of men's underwear, but none of it was mine. There were rows and rows of socks, brand new, still wrapped in their paper labels, some on little plastic hangers. I threw a little bit of everything into the bag.

Under some loose lingerie I found the wooden box where Nina kept her grandmother's jewelry. The box was fitted with a little toy lock. I didn't try to open it. I fit the box in the duffle bag and I got down on all fours and squeezed under the bed on the wall side. I saw something I couldn't reach, so I got up and went around to the side where the man was sleeping. His snores had changed. He sounded like a horse having a nightmare.

I picked up one of his big shoes to see if it were mine, which of course it couldn't be, but that's how filled with grief I was, so blind to what I was really doing there on my hands and knees. Big Red sat up. He yawned like a bear.

"What time is it," he said.

"Almost eight," I said.

He stretched his arms, swung his legs over and set his feet down next to where I was holding his shoes.

"Excuse me," he said. "Lately, it takes me forever to wake up."

I put his shoe down next to its mate and backed one giant step away. I gave him all the room he needed.

He took a couple of strong breaths sitting on the edge of the bed. He had a waist that hung down over his underwear, but he was mostly solid. He squinted in my direction then made two fists and rubbed his eyes.

"Who are you?" he said, yawning.

I didn't give him anything but a blank stare. I didn't move an inch. I watched him stretch and I got ready. His hands and arms were huge. I set myself in case he decided to charge.

He said, "You'll need to excuse my manners. I'm a slug before coffee. I'm an idiot, I apologize."

Then he sniffed the air like he was drinking it in.

"What about it? What do you say? Any chance," he said.

"Chance of what?" I said.

"Cup of java, cup of Joe," he said. "Instant's okay if that's all you got."

"The kitchen is right through there," I said and pointed.

He yawned again—a full mouth yawn that stretched his face to full capacity before he clamped down hard and turned it into a toothy smile.

"Oh, I know all about the kitchen, friend."

That's what he called me: friend.

"You see, I've been here before," he said. "I've been here dozens of times. I know my way around."

"Is that right," I said.

He stayed grinning. He had startling eyes, highly focused eyes. I liked that he might be crazy.

I bent down and closed the zipper on the duffle bag. I tugged at the handles. It had considerable weight.

He said, "I hear some fool went nuts one day and threw the coffee machine through a window. A few weeks later the same fool throws a two hundred dollar espresso maker out the window. What would you do to a fool who did those things?"

I didn't say anything, didn't move a muscle.

He said, "So, you the husband?"

I said, "Why?"

He said, "No reason. You look young, that's all."

I wanted to ask him how old I looked. I let my breath come and go in little spurts. I could feel my heart shifting gears. I let go of the duffle bag and stood up straight. I set my stance, all my weight forward. We heard the door.

I stayed focused and he held his gaze on me. He was still showing all his teeth.

He said, "If you are the husband, I respect that, friend."

"Stop calling me friend," I said. "I'm not your friend."

Nina in her heels clattered in.

"What's this?" she said.

We looked at her.

"Why are you here? What are you doing," she said to me. She stepped between us, holding a small brown paper bag. "What's he been asking you," she said to the man on the bed.

"I hope that's coffee," Big Red said.

"I'm calling the cops," Nina said.

"No cops," the man said.

Nina's purse was a round pouch on a long strap. She had it looped over her neck. "Tomorrow I'm changing all the locks," she said. "I mean it. I'm dead serious this time."

To the man she said, "Did you say anything? Because you do not want to open your mouth around this clown. Do it once and you'll regret it. Say a single word that he can use in a court of law, he will use that word. Believe me. I lived it."

"You a lawyer," the man said

I nodded.

"He's not a lawyer," Nina said. "Don't listen to him."

"Yes, I am. I have a law degree from Harvard."

"He's nuts. He's not a lawyer," Nina said. "He's not anything. He just thinks he is."

"My name is Perry Mason," I said to the man, who grinned very wide.

"Is that my coffee, baby," he said to Nina. "Please say yes. I need my coffee, sugar."

"Light and sweet," she said, and touched his cheek with the back of one finger. She handed him the bag. "Sleep good?"

"I slept wonderfully," the man said. "Only the dead sleep better than me. You know what I'm saying to you, friend?"

Nina had lost weight, a lot of it from her face. She had sharp edges again. Her hair was pulled back tight and she was wearing tiny gold earrings that looked like wedding bands.

"You hear what I am saying, friend?"

She looped her arm around his neck. "He's not listening to you," she said, and finger combed his beard. "I told you, he's nuts. He's not like a regular person. You have to feed him information like you feed it to a machine. Sequentially. Like this," she said, and looked hard at me. "Listen. Not that it's any of your business, but for your information I didn't sleep with Larry."

"Who the fuck is Larry?" I said.

The big man pulled a white Styrofoam cup out of the bag and raised it above his head like he was voting. "I'm Larry." He wasn't smiling now; Nina was watching his every move.

"If you have to know everything, we went out one time before. One other time before that. We danced a few dances. Last night we had a nice time. Didn't we have a good time last night, Larry?"

"We had a fantastic time last night," the man named Larry said. He peeled the plastic lid, licked the bottom.

"Last night, it got late. The roads were icy. So I invited Larry to stay," Nina said. "That's all this is."

Larry sipped and said, "She's not lying. It was a downpour. Soon as we stepped out of the car the sky opened up above us."

He dropped the lid inside the paper bag, crumpled the bag in his big hand, discarded the balled up bag behind him.

"But I didn't touch her. I swear. Not a finger."

He put a hand on Nina's back. She shifted a little, to make it easy for him to reach some spot they had an understanding about. I watched the corners of his huge mouth. He was a cheery fellow, a man happy to be alive. I could see the muscles in his shoulder moving. His hand went lower. He might have been pinching her ass for all I know. I couldn't tell anything by Nina's face. She was sitting in his lap, staring like a goof. I set my focus on a spot between their noses and waited for one of them to turn; I tried to think of what I could say to make this man want to hurt me.

He looked so goddamn content with his cup of coffee and my wife sitting on his lap, grinning at his surroundings. I felt like hitting something.

Nina said, "I'm not making excuses. I'm not. I deserve a life is all I'm saying." You're never here." She was talking to me but looking at Larry, watching him sip his coffee. "Nobody ever knows how to find you. Every week somebody tells me they heard you're dead."

Larry was scratching at his chin and looking at the floor between us. I hadn't moved in a while but I was ready to go. My legs felt solid, my arms loose. I clenched my fists, ready to go wild.

Nina said, "Don't hold your breath waiting for an explanation. You know how to use the door."

I stretched my fingers to loosen the joints, then curled my right hand into a fist. Nina kept her car keys in her purse. It was a matter of timing—a quick snatch and run.

Larry swallowed another mouthful of coffee. He was watching my feet.

"This is excellent," he said. "Just what I needed. Can't thank you enough."

I stared at his face but I couldn't tell if he was thanking me for the woman on his knee or referring to the goddamn coffee. When Nina leaned to kiss his mouth, all the muscles in my face started twitching. Will you believe me if I confess I didn't care about the kiss? It's just that I had people waiting, three dangerously serious men, and the clock was ticking. My heart rushed blood to my brain. I felt pumped, revitalized, ready to spring. I just needed one of them to look at me.

A Note to Hansel, 30 Years Late

Dear Hansel, my darling brother,

Forgive my long delay in writing to you. Just this morning I realized it's been thirty years since the incident. I do hope you are healthy and happy and have remained so since we last spoke. For what it's worth, I did send you an invitation to my wedding a couple of decades ago, though perhaps you had already moved by then and did not receive it. On the chance that hastily scribbled last minute invitation did find you, and you simply chose to ignore it, I understand. Water under the bridge, as they say. No hard feelings. No regrets. None directed towards you, at least.

Just last week I ran into someone from your neck of the woods, someone who knows you, and our history, apparently. The whole story, more or less. Though she didn't go into specific detail, thank god. Or give me any slanted looks. Or ask for my autograph, which a surprising amount of people, especially children, still do. Anyway, this woman, who had fine clothes and an impressive feathered hat, says you've lost a surprising amount of weight. An amazing amount, she said. All your 'witch's fat,' she called it, this person, who was half my age. Then she sighed and said you'd turned all your blubber into hard muscle, that you are no less handsome (she may have said 'hunky') as ever, with barely any lines (which she called 'distinguished') on your sun-bronzed face, and neat white hair instead of wild black. (No doubt thick as ever.) I didn't remember the lady from anyplace but she seemed to know you pretty well, said you had recently been hired to clear six acres of woodland for her husband. She seemed quite impressed by your work, so perhaps her husband can give you a letter of recommendation. Couldn't hurt. Though, and I mention this only because it struck me as odd, she made no mention whatsoever of the scar on your hand, or whether you still wear a glove to conceal it when you work.

I'll get right to the point, my brother. I'm finally willing to admit you had the right idea. Okay? So that's done. That thorny issue is finally settled. You know how it is. Time permits reflection. Age brings clarity, if not wisdom. No question your mind was sharper than mine back then. Scattering crumbs to mark our trail, leaving a chance for return. Wonderful idea. Clever, resourceful. Though not at all practical, which was always my point. A smarter plan would have been to collect white stones from the lakeshore and drop one every few paces. Do you remember those stones, small as sparrow eggs and just as smooth; how we thought they had value, or held some power. You named them 'lake jewels' because wet or dry they shined, even in moonlight. You could have used those shining stones to dot a trail. A pocketful of lake jewels would have changed both our lives.

Believe it or not I still have a jar full that you gave me one year on my birthday, so many birthdays ago. I can't look at them, can't hold one in my hand without becoming annoyed. I remember being so angry that fateful day, and so tired, and so goddamn hungry. It hurt my head to walk. I couldn't think. I didn't realize father was leading us deeper into the forest than he ever had before. I was cramped, frustrated, ravenous. I hadn't had my period in weeks. Naturally I balked at the sight of you wasting our chunk of bread.

But you suspected what he was up to. You knew, and you played it cool.

Incidentally, how is it people still speak of a stepmother, a supposedly wicked femme fatale who manipulated father into abandoning us? How does such a rumor still linger when everyone within fifty miles knows the fool never remarried. Because what woman in those days or even now wants a deaf and dumb ugly, drunken, worthless man?

But before I digress into my personal matrimonial woes, let me get back to the morning father carried his axe on his shoulder and we obediently followed behind, but not too close, least that silent, uncaring monster simply turn and murder us where we stood. Imagine if he had turned, while I bitched and screamed, slapped and kicked. God forgive me, but I was ready to kill you over that chunk of bread. And when you held me off, almost effortlessly, I sunk my teeth into your hand and drew blood. I never told you this but I swallowed that small piece of flesh I tore from you.

Do you forgive me that scar, my brother? Do you forgive my absence all these years?

You have to understand, I felt like an animal, probably because we had always been treated like beasts, not children. And I was fed up. I had had it. And there you were tossing bread carelessly into the dirt. My bread. My supper.

But by the time we reached deep woods, though darkness had set in, you had calmed me down and wrapped your wound, and convinced me of two things: one, a few bites of stale bread would have been a measly meal, deeply unsatisfying, and two: no one was suggesting we ever go back.

"It's just," you said, "that in life options are everything. They are everything, Gretel. Because they are all we have." Do you remember saying those words?

Even as a child you were so much smarter, seeing the world so much clearer than me.

Of course, by then we could no longer see the gleam of father's axe, or hear his feet rustling leaves, and we understood we had been abandoned, and then we discovered your trail of bread crumbs had vanished and we knew we were lost.

I remember screaming until my throat hurt, panicked by the sounds of night creatures echoing all around, and the cold gloom closing in, only the moon to warm us. I remember you making a bed of leaves, then holding me tighter than you ever had before, and I remember believing every word you told me, every whispered hope, and the warmth of your blood in my mouth as I sucked the wound I'd made in you.

So you quickly made a wound in me, tore me open with my legs on your shoulders. And when you were finished I stood up knowing nothing except that I was changed, different, bloody and confused.

What would our lives have become, I wonder, if at dawn we hadn't turned south, crossed the bridge, found that house built of confection, and the half-blind hag who locked you in a cage then forced me to clean and cook, feed you piles of fruits and cakes, one roasted creature after another? So much food for you and barely a crumb for me.

And how grotesque you became right before my eyes, slobbering away.

Do you remember the very last thing I fed you? A huge baked goose. A forty-pounder. I remember because I singed my hands tearing its flesh into junks small enough to fit through the bars, just so I could lick the fat and juices off my fingers, all the while glaring at your blubbery face sunk deep in your massively swollen neck. How I hated your appetite, and what you'd become. Not my brother, but a beast ready for slaughter.

And when that goose was devoured, instead of picking up the bones, I eyed the old hag leaning precariously into her oven, so I ran, threw all my weight into her, and shoved her bent broken body into the flames.

Do you know I still hear her screams whenever winter winds blow, that I still smell the stink of her burning flesh after every summer rain. It's in my head, I know, and I take a potion for that, but I still fall into fits of weeping, understanding it was the worst thing I ever did, shoving

111

that hag into the fire, and the absolute right thing to do, the only choice I had to save you, that daring desperate act.

And I am not sorry for any of it. Though I often wonder how you cope with that memory. Please do write soon and tell me where you keep all the memories we made, all our special secrets.

I miss you, Hansel. I miss your smile, your eyes, your smell, your voice. I miss how you would carry me piggy back or over your shoulder or cradled high in your arms. I miss the lake jewels on our long walks, and the short sprints we made to those crooks and caves and clearings that only you knew about. And how dizzy I would feel when we left them.

You never write, never visit. Not a word or a whisper in thirty years. Family should stay in touch.

I blame the birds. Who do you blame?

The Winter of the Frozen Moon

My name is Coleen (pronounced kuh-leen) which is an Irish term for girl, though that's the least important part of this story.

In 1970, when I was fourteen, Rhode Island got slammed by a Nor'easter that dumped two feet of snow, burying everything, closing highways, and knocking out power for about 36 hours. In the days following the storm the weather remained fiercely cold, especially at night, and all day the sky was one big dull seamless grey cloud. A rumor started that the sun had taken a holiday, gone to one of the Pacific islands and was considering never coming back. It was a joke, of course. People laughed when someone said it. But I began to wonder if perhaps it was true, because more snow came. Another small storm hit every other day. Whatever had been cleared or shoveled had to be cleared and shoveled again. The air became so cold that the snow was a fine, dry powder that wouldn't stick to anything, not even itself. Every day I used a broom to sweep the cement steps and walkway. The wind gusted and the cold stung my face and the snow swirled like dust, sometimes making shapes that rose from the ground and moved around me like ghosts. And whenever I looked at the sky I saw that the moon was always in the same place. I began to suspect that the moon had frozen solid in the sky. At first I wasn't convinced, so I kept checking. I used a soft-tipped marker to draw a circle on the kitchen window to measure the spot. And every time I looked I felt sick. Day or night the moon remained within my circle.

I mentioned this to no one, of course, not even my mother, who already had enough to worry about. And I suspected it was bad manners to mention the frozen moon in the same way that it was improper and impolite to talk of my father's passing. I understood this because my teachers not once spoke about either event, and neither did my friends. No one mentioned the missing sun or the frozen moon on the radio or TV, not even on the nightly news with Walter Cronkite.

For a while life went on like it always does, then one Sunday we went to church. We hadn't attended a service since before my father's death. The chapel was crowded. People were squeezed into every pew. We found a spot in a middle pew. People had to move. I sat and breathed the stench of perfume and sweat. I filled my nostrils with the odor of packed humanity.

In the middle of the sermon my mother stood up and said, "That's all very good, but shouldn't we be focusing our attention on the problem at hand. Shouldn't we be working together to build a ladder long enough to reach the moon? How long are we going to sit here and pretend nothing is wrong? Shouldn't one of us volunteer to climb up there and have a good look around? Perhaps nothing can be done. But aren't we obligated to try to do something?"

During her speech a murmur of voices rippled through the congregation, but as soon as she stopped talking and sat down again the minister cleared his throat and everyone shut up. No one looked at my mother, though it felt to me like the whole world was watching. After a short silence the minister stepped away from his pulpit. He adjusted his robe as he moved down the steps of the altar. With his hands in front of him, just his fingertips touching, he came directly down the aisle, stopped at our pew, then knelt on the carpet. He clasped his hands together and silently prayed.

People had turned their heads to watch. I saw them all close their eyes to pray along with him. Then I looked at my mother and saw that her eyes were open, her jaw tight, her mouth a flat line. After a long minute or two the minister stood up and turned around. He briefly glanced at my mother and me. He had made a great speech at my father's funeral service, and another, shorter speech, when the coffin was lowered into the ground, but he didn't seem to have anything to say now. On his walk back to the altar he spread his arms and turned his hands upward, giving a signal. The organist played a sustained note and the congregation burst into song. They were still singing their heads off as my mother led me quietly out the side door.

I didn't ask what her outburst was about. I wanted to know but didn't feel it was my place to question her. I was pretty sure it had something to do with my father. Usually, right after church, we hiked across town to the cemetery to stand and stare at his grave for twenty or thirty minutes. A small plaque marked the spot. The plaque looked like metal but if you touched it you could tell it was plastic. My mother was supposedly saving up to buy a headstone, but it had already been fifteen months. While she stared at the ground, I scooped up a handful of snow and tried to pack it into a snowball, but it wouldn't hold its shape. I tried again with snow scraped from the foot of my father's grave and my mother said, "Stop doing that. You're making it look like hell."

That night I fell asleep on the couch with the TV on and had a dream where my mother and I built a ladder out of fallen trees. It was a sturdy ladder, though it didn't seem long enough to reach the moon, but as we climbed the rungs it just kept going and going, sort of unfolding upward as we climbed. The moon's surface was grey, not white. We still couldn't find the sun, but there was some light, enough for us to see our shadows, and the atmosphere felt warmer than the Earth. I was excited, ready to look around the place, maybe find the spot where the astronauts had planted an American flag, and left overlapping footprints. But we just stood there, holding hands and looking at the stars, waiting to be saved, to be filled with the holy spirit, to feel better about ourselves. Overall it was a good dream, a soothing dream, except for the end, when I got tired of waiting for salvation, and understood that no one, especially not my father, was going to climb up and join us. So I let go of my mother's hand, and that was a mistake, because as I drew the ladder up, planning to break it down and turn it back into trees, I saw my mother floating off, growing smaller, like she was falling into a hole.

I bounded off the couch, panicky but alert. The TV was off but there was enough light from the kitchen to guide me. I found my mother in her bed, on her side, her legs drawn up. She was lying on top of the covers, wearing a nightgown, silky and white. She looked like a princess from a fairy tale or a bride on her wedding night. I climbed onto the bed and snuggled up to her back, rested my hand on her shoulder, my body following the same shape as hers. I started to feel warm, then feverishly hot. I think it was the smell of her, combined with the heat of her thighs against my legs. I thought it best to roll away from her, and lay on my back. After a few deep breathes I began to relax. I closed my eyes and a gentle downiness fell over me. I thought about my dream, my dead father, the frozen moon, the vacationing sun, about the coldness in the silence of strangers, and the harshness of the cruelty in their stares. But none of that bothered me because for the first time in a long time I felt safe, secure, protected, and I let my mind drift until it settled into a deep thick dreamless sleep. Would you believe me if I claimed that when I woke up I was a different person entirely? Would you understand if I said that on winter nights when there is no moon—whether drunk, sober, alone or in anyone's embrace—I have not slept so soundly since?

115

The Messenger

Now that my sciatica pain has dulled to where I can sit in a chair like a normal person and breathe without wincing, I'm telling my troubles to Mabel over loose-leaf chamomile tea. Not because I like chamomile, or because I necessarily need a second opinion (Mabel promised to read the tea leaves and predict my future once we're done,) though I suppose it never hurts to hear another woman's take on a difficult situation, especially a psychic neighbor who's got a spare room with a pullout couch. The immediate reality is Jimmy's gone, the rent is overdue, the landlord's a stubborn, selfish prick, and I need to make quick arrangements before I end up living and sleeping in the street.

So I tell Mabel, I tell her:

Forget Jimmy. Don't even mention his name. He's yesterday's news, Mabel. Good bye and good riddance. But this boy, Yiska—the half-breed I told you about—oh Mabel, what a sweet kid. Not only could he work the grill faster than Jesus Christ himself, pushing out orders like a machine, but every morning, in that forty-minute lull we get between breakfast and lunch, he'd make for me a flower out of nothing but toilet paper.

Toilet paper, Mabel. You had to see it to believe it. First he'd separate all the tissues into a stack of squares, each one offset a little from the rest, and press them in an accordion fold. If he held it by one end it looked sort of like those little Chinese fans you get when you buy Chinese food. He'd pinch the middle with one of those twisty things that come on the bags of bulky rolls and make this little scrunched up bow-tie, then he would start peeling and curling up the edges one at a time.

It was an amazing thing to witness.

He'd concentrate so hard, licking his fingertips between pulls, curling a petal at a time, fluff the whole thing out and just like magic that little stack of toilet paper bloomed into a flower.

"For you, Emily," he'd say. "To wear in your wonderful hair."

I admit my heart raced with each presentation. Anyone could see the great amount of work involved.

But then it got to be an everyday thing, and a regular joke among the other girls. And not just a friendly tease, but snide, vicious remarks, even though I'd never dream of actually putting anything made of toilet paper on my head. It was a neat trick but any fool could see they weren't real flowers.

116

Some days I'd find one in my tip glass and I'd have to pretend I hadn't noticed while behind the grill Yiska eyed me, smiling each time I put in an order. I didn't smile back, not because I'm a snob, but because he was just a kid and I didn't want him to get the wrong idea.

After a while, it got to be a bit too much. One day I walked over to the cash register and I told Matt about it. Matt's the manager and he runs a tight ship. He took the kid aside and told him to knock it off. "Stop wasting all my god damn toilet paper," Matt said.

I was sitting one booth over, listening, but basically minding my own business. Matt's tone made me queasy. I didn't want the poor kid to get fired.

He warned Yiska that technically and legally he was pilfering paper goods. "Keep it up and I'll have to start charging you."

Later, during the rush, I heard Yiska shout, "Hey Matt! How much?"

He was grinning at me, holding a platter of fries just out of my reach.

"How much for what?" said Matt from the register.

"How much you want to dock my pay for toilet paper."

"Hell, I don't know," Matt said. "Ask me later. I'd have to figure it out. I'd need to check prices and stuff."

"Do the math," Yiska said, winking. "If it is not too much, maybe I buy a case and turn all that toilet paper into pretty flowers."

I tell Mabel all this, then pause to sip my tea which has gone cold. She picks up her spoon and stirs the leaves at the bottom of her cup. Then she squeezes her eyes shut to show me she's considering my situation on a whole other level.

These last few days, Mabel's been the closest thing to a friend that I've had in years. I like that she doesn't own a TV or a hi-fi, doesn't have a car or a license to drive. She lives on fresh fruit and vegetables and every night she curls her own hair. She's a reader who goes through two, sometimes three books a week—some of them thick as the phone directory. While she's considering the depth of my situation, I'll share the part of my story she already knows, though, to be honest, there's more to tell than I have patience for.

The first bad thing that happened was right after Easter Jimmy's mother died. I never met the woman. She was seventy-one, and sickly, but still, death is always such a shock, especially around a holiday. Her name was Margaret, and she never had much. And she didn't leave much. Just Jimmy, a few distant cousins, a sister in the nut house, and a small life insurance policy. Jimmy made me pick through her things before bagging them for Goodwill. There were a couple of pretty dresses, but they were old as hell with ribbons and lace and they weren't my size. Jimmy didn't skimp on the funeral. He did it all first class, which was truly a waste seeing only a handful of people showed. After he received the insurance check he paid the mortician, got what was left over, and we finally caught up on the rent.

That was a relief.

I thought maybe our luck was changing when Jimmy hit on a couple of scratch tickets. Nothing big. But it was enough to get the phone turned back on. For once it looked like we might get back on our feet, then my sciatica started up. I felt it coming, so I went right into what Jimmy calls "sciatica mode." I got out my good girdle, quit wearing heels, and rode the bus back and forth to work. At night all I did was lie dead on the couch, watch TV, and chew on baby aspirin. Jimmy was a peach. He waited on me hand and foot. He did the grocery shopping, fried me an egg or heated up a can of soup if I wanted. He moved the rabbit ears around when I needed a channel changed. And right before he'd go to bed, he'd bring me my tea and a goodnight kiss.

It was the shifts at the diner, all that time on my feet, that did me in. The burning in my spine gradually moved into my hips and down to my legs. I had wild spasms. I couldn't lift a tray without crying. At home I just stayed on the couch like a corpse hoping that would do the trick. I chewed so much aspirin I could hear my toes tingling.

Mornings I'd wake up so stiff and cramped I couldn't comb my own hair, couldn't fix my own makeup, couldn't tie my own shoes. I had become a woman twice my age. On my way out I'd stop outside Mabel's door and have her tie my laces and fix my lipstick. Mabel's on the first floor and leaves her door open so she sees everything. She's got a police scanner and she hears all the news.

Before Jimmy popped into the picture, Mabel helped me out with a couple of small loans. She got a disability check the third of every month. She didn't like Jimmy but when he wasn't around or wasn't looking she'd still slip me a few bucks.

At work, I couldn't sit very long, so on my breaks I'd stand out back by the dumpster with the girls who smoke. Some days I'd nibble at a sandwich. Matt didn't care. He'd scream and yell at the other girls, but not me. I'd wait for the counter to fill up. Between orders I'd press against the ice machine, tug the back of my skirt up, and that helped.

Matt must have let on. Soon everybody knew why I wasn't smiling. My regulars took it okay, but a lot of stragglers who didn't get super service stiffed me. Maybe they thought I was wincing at the food.

Then one Friday some lady wearing enough jewelry to open her own jewelry store leaves a lousy nickel beside her soup cup. A nickel!

I almost walked out that day.

I was heading for Matt's little office, when Yiska pulled me aside and gave me some pills. Little football shapes, a whole baggy full. The baggy was attached to a small bouquet of paper flowers.

"What are these," I said.

He smiled. "Take two, never more than two. For pain."

I still don't know what they were but they got me through another week.

Yiska's full name was Yiska Brown Tree Margarita (spelled just like the drink) and he was a handsome boy—one third Navajo, one third Mexican, one third something else. Dark eyed with a wide nose and lips too full and too pretty for a boy. I was old enough to be his mother but he kept asking me for a date. He wanted to take me dancing. He said I had the legs of a dancer.

I told him to stop making flowers out of toilet paper.

He said he would.

Then he asked me if I'd like to run away with him.

I said sure, great, why not, I said. Just don't plan on it to be tomorrow or the next day, I said Because my boyfriend wouldn't like that.

That changed his tune. The mention of a boyfriend halted his production of paper flowers and ended his comments about my legs.

Barely a smile after that.

I felt bad. I felt sorry for the kid. Probably the worst thing about Yiska was he acted like working at the Cup N' Saucer was the best job in the world.

The day I threw my apron down he blew me a little kiss from behind the grill.

I knew what I was doing. Jimmy had landed himself a job painting houses for the summer and I was taking an immediate and long overdue vacation. The money wasn't much but it covered the rent and the phone, with a few bucks left over for groceries. On a really big job, say, a mansion, we'd have to wait till the end of the week, and then it would usually be a check with taxes already taken out. But most days Jimmy got paid under the table, in cash, and every night he turned it over just like clockwork. He didn't raise a fuss about handing it in, or give me a hard time over him earning it. And he didn't try and hold back any, either. At least none that I knew about.

The main thing is he was trying. Anyone could have seen that.

He still liked his beer on the weekends, but he'd given up on the other stuff, just like he'd said he would. A few months earlier, in a scene out of a motion picture, he'd promised his dying mother he'd change for the better, and he had, and she'd been wrong about him. He was being so nice, I sometimes handed back a few bucks and told him to go have a party. I thought his mom would have liked that. He'd been good almost a year.

Then, in June, a terrible thing happened. Out of the blue Jimmy's daughter called. To this day I don't know how she got the number or how she found out who Jimmy was living with. Nothing was in his name—not the phone, not the electric, nothing. I'd never met the woman. I could have tripped over her in the street and not known who she was. The only picture Jimmy had showed a pretty teenager with a long face and braided hair, braided like two short ropes, and God, that picture must have been eight, nine, almost ten years old. He hadn't spoken to her once in the two years we'd been together. Sometimes when he got really bad and feeling sorry for himself, he'd take out that picture and sit in the big chair. He'd sit there and rock himself to sleep. It didn't do no good to talk to him.

The thing about Penny was legally she wasn't Jimmy's daughter anymore. Long before I'd hooked up with him, Jimmy's ex had fixed his wagon in that respect. And she'd fixed it good. With the law on her side she'd nailed Jimmy for nonsupport, abandonment, and contempt of a court order. Then she and her new husband pushed through an adoption, terminating Jimmy's parental rights once and for all. When Jimmy sobered up six months after the fact, he visited a lawyer. He was furious. He brought the papers the sheriff had delivered to his mother's house. He wanted the lawyer to drag his ex into court so he could tell his side of it. The lawyer looked into the matter and in the end didn't charge Jimmy a nickel because there was nothing he could do. It was too late for an appeal. "Why didn't you answer the summons?" he asked Jimmy. "Why didn't you contest the adoption? Why didn't you pay something here and there? Something. Anything."

"I was sick," Jimmy told him, which was a line he'd picked up from AA. He never told people about his fight with the pipe, or the months he played with needles, or the money he stole from god knows where.

"Substance abuse. You could have explained that to the court," the lawyer said. "You could have gotten a postponement. We could have fought this thing if you'd come to me then."

"Cut to the chase," Jimmy said. "What can I do now?"

"Now? Now you're fucked," the lawyer said. "Now you can go on telling yourself she's still your daughter. I'm sorry," the lawyer said. "The law is the law, but it doesn't mean anything. You know in your heart she's your flesh and blood. I'm sorry, I can't help you."

That's the way Jimmy tells it. And the lawyer was right, the law is the law, but the human heart is something different and apart. So that's what Jimmy did. He took the lawyer's advice. He went on believing Penny was still his daughter and years later when he read in the paper she'd gotten married he called her up to congratulate her. That was about a month before I met him.

Jimmy called and the new husband answered and Jimmy said, "Hello. Is Penny there?" When she came on the line, he said, "Congratulations on your wedding, sweetheart. I hope everything works out for you. I love you very much and I'm going to send you a little something as soon as my ship comes in."

Penny said, "Who is this, please?" and Jimmy said, "It's me. It's your father. Your real father."

And then the line went dead. I don't know what Jimmy was expecting but I don't think he expected her to just hang up on him with not so much as a thank you.

He kept calling back, but the line was always busy. He tried for days and eventually a recording told him the number had been changed. Jimmy figured the new husband had changed it. Or maybe his ex had put them up to it.

He's told this story so many times I sometimes think we were together then, that I was right by his side. Once I dreamed Penny invited me to her house, just me, not Jimmy, and while I was there Jimmy called and got through on the new number. In my dream Penny looked just like her picture, same long face, same braided hair, except she was wearing a wedding gown. The gown's train was twenty or thirty feet long and it had gotten caught in a door. People were outside banging and screaming to get in, and the phone was ringing and Penny was crying and begging for someone to please answer the phone which she couldn't reach. She said she knew it was her father, her real father, and she needed to talk to him. So I walked across the dream and picked up the phone. I pulled, trying to move the receiver over to Penny but the cord wouldn't reach. Meanwhile she was tugging at her gown, running in place and getting nowhere, and I was stretching the cord as far as it would go, afraid it might snap. The whole time people outside kept banging so hard the whole house vibrated. Finally, I put the phone to my mouth and told Jimmy he'd have to call back. "It's no good, baby," I said. "Penny's gown is caught in the door. This won't work. Not today."

As I told him this I looked in a mirror which was just like a mirror in a department store, three-sided and set at angles. Penny was crying and Jimmy was crying and all of a sudden I burst out laughing, looking at myself reflected three ways. I'd never met Jimmy's ex but in the dream I was suddenly her, or what I imagined she looked like anyway. And I was laughing because I didn't want the phone to reach. I was Penny's mother, Loretta, and I didn't want Penny to talk to Jimmy. The worst thing about that dream was watching myself in those mirrors, wearing Loretta's face, and laughing like a demon I once saw in a horror movie.

My friend, Mabel, interprets dreams, so I told her about that one and asked what she made of it. She got out her dream book and started flipping through it.

"Wedding gown," she said, and wrote something down.

"Telephone," she said, and scribbled some more.

"Mirror, Door, Crying. What else?" she said.

She went on and on, making a list, looking things up and writing. Finally she put the book down and studied what she had written. She rolled her tongue around the inside of her mouth, and bit at the eraser on her pencil. She said the dream meant I was jealous.

"Jealous?" I said. "Of who? That bitch of a mother?"

"Nope," she said. "You're jealous of Penny." She pointed at my face with her pencil. "You fear the love Jimmy has for his daughter is greater than the love he has for you. It's plain as the nose on your face." She pushed the book at me. "Check for yourself if you don't believe me."

I flipped through the book which was set up sort of like a dictionary. I looked up some of the words that Mabel had written down, but I couldn't make heads or tails out of it. Every word had twenty or more single word definitions with page numbers in parentheses so you could go look them up too. I decided Mabel didn't know what she was talking about. I handed her the book and said, "Thank you, Mabel. As usual you've been a big help."

But what I really thought was she had some nerve telling people she could interpret their dreams with a dumb book she'd picked up at a flea market. Messing with a person's dreams is dangerous business, and I began to think Mabel was dangerous, too.

When Penny phoned out of the blue, the first thing I thought was: The ex is dead. Bye bye Loretta. I'm not mean-spirited but the idea didn't seem like such a bad thing. I didn't know the woman, but I'd heard enough about her to write a book. If she were dead and Jimmy hadn't killed her, all the better. Then I remembered my dream. It shot into my brain like a bullet. I moved the phone from one ear to the other. I suspected Mabel, who I'd been avoiding, of pulling some sort of gag.

"Hey," I said, "How do I know this is really Penny?"

She said, "I'll give you my number. Please tell my father to call me. Tell him it's very important. Do you have a pen?"

I jotted down the number and felt a little ashamed. The more she spoke, the more I could tell she'd been crying. Maybe somebody had died, or was getting ready to. I didn't know enough about it. And it wasn't my business. I read the number back to her, then I said I'd give Jimmy the message. "He's out painting a mansion right now," I said.

"Oh?" she said, and I heard her make a sound like she was blowing her nose.

"That's what he does," I said, "your father. He's a painter. He's always painting."

"You mean like an artist?" Penny said.

I laughed. "No, I mean like a real painter. Right now he's working on the old mansion on High Street. Do you know where that is? They're making it into a nursing home."

"I see," Penny said. "Well, please tell him to call me as soon as he can." She rattled off the number one more time and I checked it against what I'd written.

"Don't worry. I've got it. P-E-N-N-Y," I said.

What did I know? People drop dead every day. Once, when I was thirty, I was on a bus working an emery board across my nails and an old woman sat down next to me. I'm no snob so when she started talking I put the emery board away. I felt good about my life in those days. I had a nice job as a hostess at a first class restaurant in a Holiday Inn. My hair was always done up nice and I usually wore a dress with nylons. My sciatica was just beginning to act up and I had started carrying my heels in a little bag and wearing flat shoes wherever I went.

The old woman had shoes just like mine, same color and style. I noticed them when she sat down and I stared at them while she talked. She must have seventy if she was a day. She seemed pretty nervous, and kept jumping from one subject to another—the weather, the dirty bus, her grandson in the Navy. She asked if I had children and I smiled. I told her I wasn't married. She didn't believe that. "A pretty girl like you," she said. And I was pretty then, though a long way from being a girl.

To change the subject, I asked about her shoes. I moved one foot next to hers and wiggled my toes so she could see I wasn't crazy. She thought that was a riot. She wiggled her foot and we laughed. We laughed until her teeth fell out. They plopped right into her lap.

I gasped. I didn't want her to feel bad so I turned my head. I pretended to look out the window for a while. She was silent, and I gave her lots of time. Shops and people and parked cars flew by. I decided she might have to squeeze some adhesive on them.

When I turned back around her dentures were still in her lap and she was dead. I didn't know it then, of course. Her head was slumped left and I figured she'd dozed off, or else she was pretending to be asleep because of her teeth. The next day Andy, the regular driver, told me he'd found the body. He said it was a woman and I knew right away who he meant because he said the police had put her teeth in a zip-lock bag.

"Why'd they do that?" I asked.

He shrugged. "Evidence, I guess."

After Penny hung up, I thought it might be something like that. I had a bad feeling. Why else would she call? Someone was dead or someone was dying. I was sure of it. From the way she sounded it could have been her. Or her mother. Or maybe Penny needed a blood transfusion, or a kidney donor, something only Jimmy could supply. I got out of my nightgown and into some shorts and a blouse. I wrapped my hair in a bandanna and put on some lipstick. My lower back burned like someone had stabbed a pitchfork in there. Before I left I swallowed a mouthful of whiskey from a bottle Jimmy didn't know about. The whiskey helped some, but, when I hit the street and the hot humid air, each step sent a wave of agony along my spine.

To get to High street, you have to cross over the railroad tracks, or else walk way the hell over to Exchange Street, toward downtown, and come up the other side. Either way there's a stretch of uphill climbing I wasn't looking forward to. Bridges frighten me, always have, so I took the longer route toward the Cup N' Saucer hoping I'd run into somebody who'd give me a lift. It was half past two and the lunch shift would be getting out. About a block away from the restaurant I caught a glimpse of myself in a jewelry store window. I stopped to adjust my bandanna. I thought about putting on fresh lipstick and decided it wouldn't help. I looked like an old woman about to keel over from a stroke.

Up ahead I saw a couple of girls in uniforms and aprons come out of the restaurant. They stood under the coffee cup shaped sign and lit cigarettes. They seemed confused about which way to go. I recognized the hair on one of them, and, when they started toward me, I crossed over. The one I recognized didn't have a car anyway, and I didn't feel like chatting. I ducked into an entrance way of a bookstore and waited till they'd passed on the other side. I was standing there, watching them, seriously thinking about a taxi, when a green car pulled over and somebody tooted the horn. Without thinking twice I bent to see who it was and nearly fell over from the pain. It was like I'd stepped into the path of a flame thrower or something. I closed my eyes a moment, trying to find a position I could deal with. When I opened them, Yiska, the cook, was running over to me. "Emily?" he said. "Is that you?"

He didn't sound so sure.

I nodded, sucking deep breaths. I was trying to ride out the spasms.

"Jesus, Emily, I almost didn't recognize you." He came right up to me and put his arms out but he didn't touch me. My knees were trembling, and I might have been crying. He held his hands like he was measuring something. I looked at his shoes, black, spotted with grease stains. There was a piece of lettuce stuck to the toe of one. I winced.

"You look like you need a ride, Emily."

I straightened up as best I could and he finally put his hands down. He looked over at his car, then up and down the street, and then he looked at me. "I can't stay there, so if you want a ride you better get in." He smiled at my legs. "You want me to carry you?"

"I can make it," I said.

He went over and stood by the car. I managed a baby step. He looked handsome there with his high cheekbones and his hair tied back in a ponytail. I took a few more steps and he opened the passenger door. He stood there, holding the door and smiling in the heat.

A few people had stopped to watch, but now that I was moving again, they walked past. A woman with a baby carriage made a face as she steered around me.

Yiska put his arm across the opening and I held his wrist, easing myself in. The pain in my back had leveled, but now I had a headache and my mouth was dry. It felt like I had dirt on my tongue but every time I pinched the spot nothing was there. I licked my lips and tried to smile as Yiska slid behind the wheel. He put on sunglasses and started us going.

"Where to, Emily?"

"High Street," I said. "Left at the light, and straight up the hill."

"As you wish, señorita."

The inside of his car smelled just like the Cup N' Saucer. I put my arm out the window and held onto the door, looking down at the river as Yiska drove us up the hill. As we drove, I felt his eyes on my legs.

"You find another job?" he said.

I gave him a look. "Are you kidding?" I said. "I may never work again."

The house that everyone called The Mansion was actually two houses connected by a narrow addition. On the left was a Queen Anne with a wraparound porch, a high, pointed tower, and fish-scale shingles that reminded me of gingerbread. The house had been painted a week before, a bright apple green with mustard yellow trim, but it still looked wet in the afternoon sun. On the right sat an older, box shaped structure with a flat roof and door-size windows and lots of plywood. A wrought iron fence surrounded the roof. There were ladders and scaffolding set up along one side. On the lumpy lawn a huge sign told everyone "Coming Soon: Riverview Nursing home." I spotted Jimmy on the roof with a half dozen other men. They were smoking and looking out at the polluted river.

"Here. Right here," I said to Yiska, and he banged on the brakes. A pain shot up to my neck.

"Sorry," he said. He glanced at the houses and gently bumped the car onto the curb.

"This is good," I said. But the car was at an angle and I couldn't get the door open.

"I'll help you," Yiska said, and got out. He ran past the windshield and I wondered what he'd have done if I'd ever said yes to one of his proposals. He opened my door and I swung my legs out in slow motion. He grasped both my hands. "Ready," he said.

I nodded and he pulled me to my feet. Two stories up Jimmy flicked his cigarette over the fence.

"Thank you, Yiska," I said. "Never would have made it here without you."

He grinned like a school boy. "The señorita is quite welcome," he said.

I leaned against the car, trying to catch my breath.

"You want me to wait for you?" Yiska said.

"Oh, no. Thank you," I said. "I'll be all right now."

"You sure?" He tilted his head to one side and his pony tail flopped across his shoulder. He seemed to be studying my face. Then he turned and looked up at the men on the roof. "You live there?"

I smiled. "Not yet." I pointed to the sign.

He banged the heel of his hand against his forehead. "Stupid," he said, and rolled his eyes.

Then Jimmy yelled down to us. "Emily," he said. "What's the matter?"

I put my hands to my mouth, making a funnel. I shouted through them: "Come down a minute."

"I can't," Jimmy said. "What is it? What's wrong?"

I looked at Yiska who was shielding his eyes against the sun. He looked like an Indian scout from some old western. "Come down here a minute! I've got a message for you!"

"You've got a what?" he yelled.

"Somebody called for you," I said. "Can't you come down?"

"No," he said. "There aren't any stairs!" He shrugged. Then he put his arms up like Jesus Christ blessing the whole world. "Can't it wait?" he said.

I reached into my pocket and pulled out the slip of paper with Penny's phone number. I waved it above my head so he'd know I really had something. "It's from someone you know! She said it's important!"

"Well, I can't come down now," Jimmy yelled. He looked over his shoulder. He said something to whoever was there. Then he waved both arms over his head like he was signaling a plane. "I've got to go back to work now. We'll talk later, okay." He put his arms down. I waved the note and started to say something but Jimmy moved out of sight.

"Give it to me," Yiska said and showed me his hand.

I stared at his face.

"It's alright, Emily," he said. "I'll bring it right to him." He smiled. "And I won't read it."

I handed over the paper and he folded it once, then rolled it into a tiny tube. He put one end in his mouth and bit down. "Wait here," he said through his teeth. He looked at the building a moment. And then he took off, running across the yard, leaping over mounds and ditches. He ran up to a ladder that stretched to the second story windows. He climbed it till he reached a narrow platform. He walked along it like a tightrope walker, arms out, watching his footing. Midway, he stopped, looked up, then leaped across a small gap to the next platform. He followed that one to another ladder. He scurried up to a cross section of

127

pipes supporting a small platform with buckets and drop clothes. A long ladder led straight to the roof. He turned and waved at me. I waved back. He looked like he was smoking a cigarette, like he was working there. He climbed that ladder to the wrought iron fence surrounding the roof. He held on to the fence with one hand and waved the note above his head. A fat man came over, but Yiska didn't give him the note. He pointed across the roof. The fat man turned, calling out, "Jimmy! Jimmy, get your lazy ass over here!"

While he was waiting—hanging there—Yiska looked down again and waved. I didn't do anything. I wanted to, but I knew if I did he'd fall. I leaned against the car and bit the inside of my cheek.

After a few seconds, Jimmy's head and shoulders appeared. The fat man said something to him and Jimmy stepped up close to the fence. Yiska handed him the note. I turned away. I couldn't look anymore. My back hurt too much. Pain was shooting through me every which way.

I opened the car door and eased myself down to the seat. I laid back with my face near the steering wheel and my legs sticking half out the door. I could feel the sun on my ankles but the back of my legs felt all tingly. I laid there and wondered if Yiska had any more of those football-shaped pills or some other kind of pill that would make me happy.

On the ride home, Yiska told me he was leaving Rhode Island and moving back to Arizona. He said he'd saved up enough money to do what he wanted. I regret I didn't take the time to ask what that was.

Outside my house he said he was sorry I'd never gone out with him, then he wished me all the luck in the world. "You know, with your back and your boyfriend," he said.

He asked for my phone number. But I wouldn't give it to him, so he read the number on the house, and wrote down my street address on the back of his hand. He said, "I'll send you a post card. A pretty picture. Okay?"

I didn't look back. I focused on the porch railing. When I got my hand on it, Yiska blared the horn. "In Navajo my name means 'night has passed.' So maybe when I go home I will get a new name. Good luck to you, Emily! Maybe I see you again some fine sunny morning."

Mabel argued up and down that Yiska's name meant something else entirely. She claimed to have a book about names and meanings, and spent fifteen minutes on her knees looking for it. But she couldn't find it and I didn't talk to her for nearly a week, until the night Jimmy moved his stuff out. That bastard took the TV, which I'd paid for.

Mabel says, "Sweetheart, you are better off without that TV. And twice better off without a lazy man in your bed."

I don't admit to her I'll miss my programs, especially my day time shows.

"Starting tomorrow, we'll make ourselves a timetable," Mabel says.

"A timetable?"

"A schedule to keep us on track. When we'll read, when we'll shop. When we'll prepare meals, take our walks, all that," Mabel smiles.

I nod at Mable then frown at my tea.

If I had it to do over again, I'd never have given Jimmy that message.

Mabel says what I should have done is snipped the wire and thrown the phone away.

"Get behind me, Satan," she says, thumping the table, making the teacups jitter and chime.

"I get worked up just thinking about the two of them living in some fancy house on the east side. Tell me that's a normal relationship, a grown man, almost fifty, living with his divorced kid."

Mabel shakes her fist. "Nothing normal about it."

"Oh, don't I know it, too. I told him, right to his face. You should have heard me. I said Jimmy, I don't care what you do. And I meant it. You're not my friend, I said. And then I didn't wish him any luck. Good or bad. Do you know what I said to him? I said, I'll miss my god damn TV more than you. That wiped the dumb look off his face."

"Phones, TVs, and automobiles," Mabel says, shaking her head. "They're more trouble than they're worth. You buy them hoping they'll take trouble away, make life a little easier, maybe bring some joy. But it's a trap, honey. Same as living with a man. In the end all they give you is heartbreak, grief and sorrow. Usually right after you've made all the payments."

Mabel knows what she's talking about. She's got a new book, a fat hardcover we picked up from the two-for-a-quarter table. The title is *Tomorrow's Consumer Confluence* and it's all about the future. "Someday soon," Mable says, "so fast it'll set our heads spinning, AT&T or Mobil-Exxon or Microsoft, maybe Wal-Mart—one of those bastards is going to pack everything into one neat little bundle that they'll jam right down our throats. No more cars, no more computers, no more TVs and telephones. You watch," she says, lifting my cup away. "We'll all be living in our own little high-tech plastic bubbles, drifting aimlessly around, sucking food through a straw and reading one another's minds."

I tell Mabel I'm eager for the world to change. I tell her I can't wait.

Acknowledgements

"Beauty Takes Care of Itself," *Pulp Literature*, issue 6, 2015. Editor's Pick. 2016 Pushcart Nomination.

"Blue Light" appeared in *Zoetrope All-story-Extra*, Issue 26: September 2000.

"Significance of Sunlight" appeared in *Night Train*, issue 7.1, 2007.

"Belly Breathing" appeared in the Winter 2010 issue of *The Indiana Review*.

"Oh, Alison!" received Second Prize in *Orchid's* short fiction contest, and appeared in *Orchid* #6, August 2006.

"If You'd Like To Make A Call," was awarded The Barry Hannah Fiction Prize, and originally appeared in *The Yalobusha Review*, 2007. It was later republished by *Pulp Literature*, 2016 and nominated for a *Pushcart Prize*.

"At The Factory" received First Prize in *Rumble Underground's* 2007 Fiction contest, and appeared in *Rumble Underground*, 2007.

"Tomorrow Isn't Friday," appeared in *Turnrow*, Fall 2007.

"Treasure Hunt" appeared in *Underground Voices*, 2006, and was nominated for The Million Writers' award.

"All Set For Ardor?" was a semi-finalist for The 2009 Eric Hoffer Award, and was later published by *LitBreak*, January 2016.

"Newborn" appeared in *BoundOff*, an audio literary magazine, Issue 74, March 2012.

"The Next Stop" received Second Prize in *Literary Juice's* short story contest, May 2013, and later republished by *Fabula Argentea*, January 2016.

"That Whooshing Noise Before the End," appeared in *The Literarian*, Issue 9, 2012.

"Beauty Takes Care of Itself," appeared in *Pulp Literature*, Issue 6, spring 2015, and nominated for The Pushcart Prize.

"ABCDEFGH," appeared in the *Marie Alexander Poetry Series* anthology "Nothing to Declare: A Guide to the Flash Sequence," released February 2016.

"A Note to Hansel," appeared in *Boundoff*, a Short Story Podcast, Issue 104, September 2014.

About the Author

Bob Thurber is an old "unschooled" writer with no degrees in anything. Born in 1955 and raised in abject poverty, Bob graduated high school by the skin of his teeth, then spent his early adult years working menial jobs while reading obsessively and studying the craft of fiction. He served a lengthy apprenticeship, writing nearly every day for twenty years before submitting his work for publication. Since then his stories have received a long list of awards and citations, among them *The Marjory Bartlett Sanger Award* and *The Barry Hannah Fiction Prize*. Selections have appeared in over sixty anthologies and hundreds of publications, including *Esquire*. Bob is the author of *Paperboy: A Dysfunctional Novel* and three other collections of stories. He resides in Massachusetts where, despite vision loss, he continues to write every day. Visit him at BobThurber.net.